FAIR
MAIDEN

FAIR
MAIDEN

⚜ LYNN HALL ⚜

F
Hal
1996

CHARLES SCRIBNER'S SONS
NEW YORK

Collier Macmillan Canada • Toronto
Maxwell Macmillan International Publishing Group
New York • Oxford • Singapore • Sydney

Charles Scribner's Sons Books for Young Readers
Macmillan Publishing Company • 866 Third Avenue, New York, NY 10022

Collier Macmillan Canada, Inc.
1200 Eglinton Avenue East, Suite 200 • Don Mills, Ontario M3C 3N1

Printed in the United States of America
10 9 8 7 6 5 4 3 2 1   First Edition

Library of Congress Cataloging-in-Publication Data
Hall, Lynn.
Fair maiden / Lynn Hall. — 1st ed.   p.   cm.
Summary: Working at the Renaissance Fair, Jennifer finds her first love and an escape from family problems at home.
[1. Fairs—Fiction.   2. Family problems—Fiction.]   I. Title.
PZ7.H1458Fai   1990   [Fic]—dc20   90-30629   CIP   AC
ISBN 0-684-19213-6

FAIR MAIDEN

Early autumn. The air was damp and cool against her face. White morning fog swirled around her, its separate particles as visible as tiny snowflakes. Above the ground, where the fog grew sheer in the pale sunlight, rose the walls of a medieval city with corner towers and three arched gates.

She stood motionless before the walled city, the fog wrapping close around her, then wafting away to leave her exposed in a shaft of early-morning sun. She was tall and slim in a blue gown that billowed around her legs. Its bodice laced tight across her breasts, flattening them in a way that was both childlike and provocative. White sleeves billowed and gathered at her wrists. Around her shoulders moved a cloud of dark, soft hair. Her face, rather plain in its setting of gown and hair, was at this moment illuminated.

She moved toward the three gates, then hesitated, turned, and looked back toward the broad meadow from which she had come. Sounds came to her through the fog, the slamming of a car door, a scolding voice, and overhead the roar of a jet lifting from the airport.

A shaft of sunlight burned through the fog and spotlighted a concession booth just opening for business, with shirts and sweatshirts and billed caps all bearing, in ornate script, the legend Minnetonka Renaissance Fair.

Jennifer Dean turned away from the sight, gathered her blue gown's hampering fullness in her fingers, and approached the gates. From overhead a voice called to her.

"Virgin gate over here, miss. Virgins only, through this gate."

She tilted her head and looked up. On the top of the wall just over the third gate perched a slightly built young man in tights and a leather vest. In his arms he cradled a wooden bucket.

"Virgins only, through this gate," he called again. "I pour boiling oil on imposters."

Jennifer grinned up at him and, holding up her skirts, ran beneath him and through the gate. No boiling oil poured down from his bucket. But then, of course, she wasn't an imposter, she reminded herself. Her virginity was genuine and she intended to keep it that way, for now.

Before her lay a broad, empty grass avenue lined with tiny plank-and-plaster shops with signs jutting

2

out above their doors. In the distance the avenue widened around an ancient oak tree, became a village green, then wandered in three directions down narrower shop-lined lanes.

It was familiar to Jennifer, who had been coming to the Renaissance fair every September for the past four years, spending as much time and money as she could. The fair woke fantasies and emotions in Jennifer that nothing in her life could match except her discovery of the movie *Camelot*, of which she owned a videotape.

Until now she had been a visitor like all the other thousands of tourists who came to the Renaissance fair during its six weekends of life, Labor Day weekend through mid-October. But beginning this morning, this first day of the first weekend of the season, Jennifer belonged to the fair.

Footsteps and voices around her brought Jennifer back to reality. She turned and went into the fair office near the entrance gate and said to the young woman at the nearest desk, "Jennifer Dean, fair maiden."

"Right. Jennifer." The woman made a check mark on her clipboard list and said, "You know what to do, don't you? Just wander around, smile and talk to people, sound as authentic as you can, and be as pleasant and helpful as possible. You know the locations of all the rest rooms and the first-aid building, don't you? And I'd like you to help out at the jousts, if you would. Two o'clock and four o'clock every afternoon, and eight at night. You know where the jousting

3

ground is, over by the elephants? Good. Just check in with the announcer a little before two; he'll tell you what he wants you to do. Have a good time, and remember your food and drinks are free. You look lovely," the woman added, peering at Jennifer more closely. "You really fit the part, you know. Some girls just never look right in costume no matter how hard they try. You look as if you were born in the fifteenth century."

"Thank you," Jennifer said with real pleasure.

The grass avenue was filling with people as she emerged from the office. A river of tourists came through the gates and then spread and slowed to meander along the row of shops. A man bellowed and ducked away from a splash of water thrown at him from the keeper of the virgin gate.

"Boiling oil for the imposter," yelled the gate-keeper. "I know a virgin when I see one, and you ain't."

The dampened man trotted away, laughing and shaking the water off, while his wife punched at his arm.

Jennifer moved down the avenue, feeling suddenly adrift. Hours stretched ahead of her in which she would have to direct herself, and she found the prospect unexpectedly intimidating. Her life was regulated and structured, as were the lives around her. She and her mother had scheduled bathroom times in the mornings, ate their breakfasts with an eye on the clock, and spent their evenings with homework and office work done in half-hour time slots between favored television shows.

Even Jennifer's summer vacation, just ended, had been eaten away this year by fifty hours a week of hostessing at the Country Kitchen, saying, "How many for lunch? Smoking or nonsmoking? Booth or table?" It hadn't paid as well as waitressing because there were no tips, but it had been the only summer job she could find, and it had paid for the six-year-old Toyota that would take her to college next year.

This weekend and the next five weekends, during which she would play Fair Maiden as an unpaid extra at the Minnetonka Renaissance Fair, were to be her vacation, her breathing space between the Country Kitchen and her senior year at Lake Minnetonka High School. She'd have to pay for these precious weekends with extra homework during the week in order to keep her grade average where she wanted it, where it must be in order to get her into Northwestern.

But the extra work would be worth it. She knew that. She felt it as she felt the fog particles against her cheek. This fair, this fantasy world, was her true setting. She had known that from her first visit here four years ago. This fair was more vividly real to Jennifer than her school or her home, more real than her friend Kelly and, please God, more real than her brother, Michael.

It made no difference to Jennifer that the shops lining the avenue had been built in weeks instead of centuries, that the meadowland and the river behind it would, in a few years, become a concrete-and-glass industrial park and that the Renaissance fair was nothing more than a temporary income producer for the corporation that owned the land.

The fair was the only existence Jennifer wanted. She felt safe within the walls of this fake village, safer than at home with the threat of Michael, with the old pain of Chris's desertion still stabbing her in unguarded moments.

She was beyond the row of shops now, where the junction of the three smaller lanes formed an open village green around the spreading oak tree. She slowed her pace and then turned around once in a wide-armed circle like a small child dancing. Her long skirts swung away from her legs, intoxicating her with their grace and her own. She tipped her head back, closed her eyes, and smiled with uncontainable joy.

Somewhere near her music began, a soft-strummed minor-key melody that was so perfect a score for her dance scene that she wasn't startled by it. The music was supposed to be there for her. Her body swayed, her feet moved on the close-mown grass, and her arms lifted with a natural grace she had never before possessed.

A man's voice, barely above a whisper, sang, "She stepped away from me and went through the fair, and fondly I watched her move here and move there. And then she went homeward with one star awake, as the swan in the evening moves over the lake."

Jennifer opened her eyes and looked around until she saw him sitting on the lowest branch on the far side of the oak tree. The tree's trunk hid most of him; she could see only a lean, dark face and the neck of the instrument he strummed.

She stood very still, recognizing in that instant a figure who would be important in her life. She didn't question that knowledge or her certainty of it; the recognition of him was instinctive.

He dropped from the tree and came toward her, strumming the poignant melody again and singing, "Last night she came to me, she came softly in, So softly she came that her feet made no din. And she laid her hand on me and this she did say: 'It will not be long, love, till our wedding day.'"

2

They stood facing each other, not intimately close and yet a pair. His head was level with hers, his hair as dark as Jennifer's and falling smooth and straight to his collar, just curling a bit around his ears. His face was dark and narrow, with traces of old acne scars just visible on his cheeks. He might have been thirty or older.

He was as slim as the girl, his legs encased in leather tights, his body in a vest of multicolored leather patches. The white sleeves of a gauzy shirt billowed around his arms.

Something deep in Jennifer moved, shifted to make room for this man whom she didn't know, yet recognized.

He bowed low, sweeping off his cap in the gesture and swinging aside the instrument that hung on a silken cord around his neck. "Good morrow, my lady. May I present myself? I am known as John the Lutanist, at your service."

A family of tourists walked past, watching and listening. Jennifer saw nothing but the minstrel bowing before her. "And I am Guinevere," she said.

The name came automatically. It was the early form of "Jennifer," a fact that drew her to Queen Guinevere every time she watched her videotape of *Camelot*. She felt one with the tragic figure on the screen and imagined herself to be that Guinevere reborn in the twentieth century.

"Not Arthur's queen, I hope," the minstrel said, and Guinevere smiled and held out her hand in an airy gesture Jennifer Dean would have bungled.

"Not Arthur's queen, nor anyone's. I am but a humble maiden enjoying the fair. I belong to no man." Why say that? she wondered as soon as the words were out.

He took her hand as naturally and gracefully as she offered it and led her to the wooden bench that encircled the oak tree. In a pouf of skirts she sat, still holding herself more gracefully erect than Jennifer ever did.

"What is your instrument?" she asked.

"A lute, silly wench. That's why I'm called John the Lutanist, not John the Git-Picker or John the Bass Fiddler."

He smiled. His eyes were small and rather close set and deep, but when they carried his smile to Jennifer, she felt again the curious shifting of some weight low in her body. With the tip of one finger, she reached out and touched the silken wood of his lute, resting across his lap.

It was a lovely thing, shaped like a pear sliced in half, with a neck shorter than a guitar's and more steeply angled at the end. The body of the lute was rosewood, with a garland of flowers of paler wood inset around it.

Now tourists were coming in greater numbers through the entrance gates and down the grass avenue toward the tree where they sat. Jennifer supposed she should be moving on, but instead she stayed and asked for a song.

John took off his cap with a practiced motion and spun it to the ground so that it lay upside down a few feet away. He pulled from his vest pocket a five-dollar bill, a few ones, and some change, and tossed them into the cap. "Seed money," he said in a low voice.

Then he leaned back against the tree and began to strum. Startled, Jennifer realized he held a bird's claw in his hand. It was the claw that plucked the strings.

He sang "Greensleeves." Jennifer felt intensely the romance of the moment as she listened to his words. Oh, to be loved like that.

"Alas, my love, you do me wrong, to cast me off discourteously. For I have love-ed you so long, delighting in your company. And I will pray to God on high that thou my constancy may see. For I am still thy lover true. Come once again and love me. Greensleeves was all my joy, greensleeves was my delight, greensleeves was my heart of gold, and who but my Lady Greensleeves."

Jennifer closed her eyes and listened. There were no tourists gathering to listen to John's song, no jet trails in the sky or freeway against the horizon. There was only a world in which men loved women totally and forever.

Not like Chris.

She shook her head and replaced the image of Chris in her mind with the real man before her, John the minstrel who looked warmly into her eyes and sang her love songs.

When she rose to leave at the end of the song, he said, "Stay awhile. Ballads need fair maidens to be sung to."

She stayed on for almost an hour, while groups of people paused to listen to John's music and to drop money into his cap. Finally he stood, collected his cap, and tipped it, money and all, onto his head.

"Farewell, my lady," he said, and walked away.

The rest of the morning passed slowly but pleasantly. Jennifer strolled the narrow lanes that wound between picturesque little shops: a tannery where soft leather knee-high boots were made and sold, a glassblower's workshop, an open-sided, thatch-roofed shop where weavers worked at looms and sold beautiful nubbly shawls and sweaters.

She smiled at everyone whose eyes met hers and said, "Good day," or "Good morrow," as John had greeted her. In the deep pocket of her gown, she carried a map of the fair and a schedule of performances for the five open-air theaters scattered along the lanes and in the clearings at the edge of the village. It gave her pleasure to offer help and directions to people who asked or who looked lost.

By late morning she was painfully hungry, but there were so many interesting shops she had trouble deciding where to have lunch. There was the shop selling roasted dragon wings and a bakery shop selling hot cross buns and a meat shop offering stag sausages and oxen burgers. Finally she settled for a tiny shop, one that had tree-shaded benches in front of it, and ordered a shepherd's pie and cider.

The sitting down was as wonderful as the pie, which proved very good, indeed. It was a flaky pastry folded over a hash of meat, vegetables, and spices. She had to lean to the side in order not to drip its delicious juice on her gown.

Chris came into her mind as she rested on the bench. Why Chris? Why think about him now, she wondered. She had been letting her mind wander as her eyes made a casual search of the lane, looking for the lute player. Where did John eat lunch, she'd been wondering. Then suddenly Chris was there in her mind, holding out his arms to her as he used to do when she was younger.

He had been such a good father for her those three years. Her own father had been gone since she was two and had a new life and family in Fort Lauderdale, Florida. She was eleven when Chris came into

12

her life, first as Mom's new boyfriend and then, quite suddenly, as her stepfather.

Like John the Lutanist, Chris was a rather small, slight man, good looking and quick witted. He took the coltish little Jennifer under his wing literally, hugging her almost as often as she needed hugging. He helped her with school projects and took her shopping for school clothes, and listened while she talked about things Mom was too busy to bother with.

Jennifer loved him.

It lasted three years and then he was gone, driven out of the family by Michael. Chris still came back sometimes, but Jennifer's mother was not interested in remarrying the man who had been frightened off by her son.

Jackie Dean was a full-fledged yuppie single woman now, successful enough not to need a husband to pay her bills, and pretty enough to enjoy an active and varied love life. She had outgrown Chris.

Jennifer, too, healed from the wrenching loss of the man who had loved her and held her in quick fatherly hugs that nourished her soul. In the three years since Chris's leaving, she had moved from hating him for failing her, to a forced disinterest in him, and finally to a sort of forgiveness in which she could be with him for an evening of television without feeling sick with the pain of his leaving her.

This past summer she had seldom thought of him. Her mother was dating a motorboat salesman and

Chris was dating someone from his office, so he didn't drop over in the evenings anymore.

John reminds me of him, she thought, but analyzed her feelings no more deeply than that.

Time to get to work. She shook the crumbs from her skirt and headed east along the winding lane toward the jousting grounds.

3

The winding lane opened onto an area that Jennifer's map called the stock market. Here were small rope pens under the trees, holding horses and donkeys and ponies, sheep and goats, and a few head of small, shaggy Highland cattle.

A wooden cart rattled past Jennifer, drawn by a pair of oxen and carrying a load of children who stood clinging to the high sides while anxious parents walked beside the cart, hands outstretched in case a child should lose his balance. A girl, another fair maiden like Jennifer, rode across the clearing on a small gray horse that had an incredibly long mane and tail. The horse curved its neck and pranced; the girl sat elegantly erect on a sidesaddle, her long gown floating back across the horse's flank.

Jennifer paused beside the pen holding the horses

15

and ponies. A donkey just inside the pen had a tiny foal nursing at her side. The foal rolled her eye toward Jennifer but went on sucking, stamping hooves no bigger than a quarter.

Over the pen hung a sign announcing Honest Geoffrey, Horse Trader. The man who stood beaming under the sign was huge and bearded and smiling, with thumbs tucked into suspenders. He wore breeches and high boots and a full-sleeved drawstring blouse like John's.

He said to Jennifer in a booming voice, "Got a special for you, this weekend only. Terrific low-mileage war-horse, only ridden on one crusade, by a little old knight who never went over five miles an hour. Guaranteed sound as a sovereign." He slapped the shoulder of a bored-looking draft horse.

"No, thanks. I think I'll pass," Jennifer said politely. "I don't really need a war-horse."

"Gift for the boyfriend," he called after her. "Okay, then, I've got a dandy little palfrey here, just right for a young lady. Nice, smooth gaits, only been ridden by a little old seamstress who never went over five miles an hour."

Jennifer laughed, waved him off, and continued across the market green. She passed a man spraying water over an elephant that appeared to be asleep and leaning into the stream of water. She dodged around the camel-ride concession and past a hay-bale enclosure in which a boy was diving and scrambling to catch a greased pig.

She knew her way around the fair from visits on

previous years, but now she was a part of it, not just a tourist. Now for the first time she felt the atmosphere of the place like a time warp. This was reality, this fifteenth-century English village, not the modern midwestern city beyond the walls. Guinevere was totally at ease here in her home village, in spite of the oddly dressed visitors who crowded the market square.

Aware of the time, she veered left and made her way toward a white fence at the edge of the stock market. It was the tourney grounds, a long, broad strip of churned earth fenced all around with stout planks. At one end a raised platform stood decked in buntings and banners of red and gold and deep blue. A brightly colored striped awning roofed the stand.

Jennifer went along the fence and up the stairs to the platform where a man and woman sat. The woman, dressed in a purple-and-gold gown with a fur-lined robe over her shoulders, sat on a thronelike chair and wore a circlet of gold on her head. Obviously, royalty. The man was also dressed in period garb but sat behind a small table that held an inconspicuous microphone.

To him Jennifer said, "Pardon me. I'm your fair maiden. They told me to report to you and you'd put me to work."

He turned from his papers and gave her a quick up-and-down look. "Hey, terrific. The last one we had was a real dog. What's your name, honey?"

"Lady Guinevere."

"Terrific. Here's what I want you to do. You can sit

17

there beside the queen till we get started. You're her lady-in-waiting, see? Then as soon as we start the jousting, you take that tambourine over there in the corner, you take the tambourine and circulate through the crowd along the fences. Collect donations. We can't charge admission here because it's all out in the open, but we do pretty good with tambourine collections."

Jennifer picked up the tambourine and sat on the edge of the platform at the queen's feet. She shook the tambourine gently and drummed it with the heel of her hand, remembering the tambourine she'd played in the third-grade band. This one was much more ornate, with long, ribbon streamers and flowers around its rim.

She turned and looked up to smile at the queen, a tiny middle-aged woman with a round, flat face. The woman smiled back. "How did you get to be queen, if you don't mind my asking?"

The woman jerked her head toward the announcer. "Married him. He's the president of the saddle club, so I have to do all this stupid stuff. The knights who do the jousts are all from our saddle club, see, and Jerry, my husband, likes to do this announcing stuff. He does all the announcing for our horse shows. Makes him feel like a big shot."

"Shut up, queenie," Jerry growled as he switched on his mike and sent his voice out over the tourney grounds and the stock market green.

"Ladies and the rest of you, hearken up here. We're about to begin. Shut up and quit talking to one another now, or you're going to miss out. We have an important joust coming up in just about three minutes, and you're not going to want to miss this one.

"Our first contest of the afternoon will pit the famous Sir Lawrence the Lover against the equally famous but much bigger Sir Harold the Huge. Let's hear it for Larry and Harry."

The crowd clapped loudly as two horsemen appeared at the far end of the course and began riding toward the stand. The course was a long straightaway divided lengthwise by a padded barrier, shoulder high to a tall horse.

The two knights trotted forward, banners flying from their upraised lances. The horses looked like ordinary riding horses to Jennifer, but they were decked in colorful caparisons, straps, and bells so that they looked impressive.

The announcer said, "On my right, in blue-and-gold harness, Sir Lawrence the Lover, riding his charger, Cupid. Let's hear it for Lover and Cupid."

Again the crowd clapped and shouted. The knight came to bow before the queen, who bent in quite a regal motion and tapped him on the shoulder with a long-stemmed rose.

"And his opponent, Sir Harold the Huge, riding his famous charger, Unlucky. Let's have a nice hand for Huge and Unlucky."

Jennifer laughed along with the tourists as the man moved forward to do homage to his queen. He was indeed a very fat man, and his horse was the most swaybacked animal she had ever seen.

From a tape player at Jerry's elbow came a fanfare of trumpets. The knights took their places, one at either end of the course, aligned with the barrier. Sir Lawrence was at the platform end of the course, his back to Jennifer.

The music changed, giving them the signal to charge. Both knights galloped forward, but before they reached the barrier, Sir Lawrence slowed his horse, turned him, and trotted back to the platform. He drew up beside Jennifer and leaned close to murmur, "Hey, there, chickie, whatcha doing tonight? Want to go someplace quiet, share a flagon of ale? Get down and dirty?"

The crowd roared with laughter.

"You're supposed to be jousting," Jennifer told him.

"Oh, yeah. You're right." He spun his horse and signaled to Jerry for starting music. Once again the two knights charged toward each other. Once again Sir Lawrence pulled up just short of combat, veered to the side, and rode to the fence where he leaned over a pretty girl in shorts and a bikini top.

Jennifer, laughing with the crowd, picked up her tambourine and began to circulate. She felt awkward, begging for money like a street bum, but within a few minutes she was at ease, protected by the unreality of the role she played.

When she had worked her way to the end of the field and was starting up the other side, she looked up and saw John the Lutanist standing at a little distance, watching her. He was with a young man in a Scottish kilt with a bagpipe on his shoulder, but neither of them was playing. They both watched Jennifer. She had the feeling they had been talking about her.

4

The fair closed at nine o'clock. Jennifer wandered rather slowly toward the gates, watching for John the Lutanist. She imagined him appearing from behind a tree, leading her off with him to some dark, private place. Kissing her.

But he was nowhere in sight by the time she reached the gates. Smiling a little sadly, she detoured through the virgin gate, found her Toyota where she'd left it in the morning fog, and drove home.

The Lakeview Chalets were a cluster of apartments and townhouses just off Interstate 494 at the southwest edge of Minneapolis. Jackie and Jennifer Dean, and Michael, had moved there when Jennifer was in second grade. They had started in a cramped two-bedroom apartment in the cheapest of the buildings in the complex, moving up in size and luxury as

Jackie's salary rose. Now she and Jennifer had one of the compact but attractive two-level townhouses with a balcony that almost overlooked Lake Minnetonka. The buildings were of gray cedar planking, boxy and stark, with rooflines rising in one-sided slopes that ended too abruptly.

When Jennifer got home she found Kelly Green sitting on the doorstep. Kelly lived in the next building and was in Jennifer's class, two facts that in Kelly's mind added up to best friend. Jennifer had her reservations about that and was in no mood to listen to Kelly tonight, while her mind was still in another century.

"Wow," Kelly said as Jennifer got out of the car. "I love your costume. You look like the real thing, Jennie. So? How did it go? What did you do? Did you meet any neat guys?"

Jennifer unlocked the front door and went in, with Kelly trailing. Kelly was shorter than Jennifer and somewhat thickly built, with straight-chopped dirty-blond hair and green eye makeup so intense it was the focal point of her face. She tended to wear kelly green much of the time in honor of her name, but the color had an unfortunate effect on her complexion.

"It was fun," Jennifer said as she climbed the stairs to her room. She unfastened the blue gown as she went and stepped out of it in the hall outside the bathroom door. Kelly sat on the toilet lid while Jennifer showered. Then they went into the bedroom and settled on the bed, the hair dryer set on low to

23

blow the moisture but not the curl from Jennifer's hair.

"So?" Kelly demanded again. "Did you meet any interesting guys?"

Jennifer thought about John. An interesting guy? Not by Kelly's standards. He was far too old, might even be married. What was he, anyway, in real life? Did he just play at Renaissance fairs all the time or what? Did he live here in the Twin Cities area?

"You did," Kelly crowed, hitting Jennifer on the leg. "I can tell from the way you're looking. You did meet an interesting guy. Who was he? What does he look like? Did he ask you for a date or anything? What's his name?"

Jennifer wrapped her terry-cloth robe tighter around her legs and shifted the hair dryer to her other hand. "No, I didn't meet anyone."

Kelly stayed for nearly an hour, talking in her fast, high voice about the start of their senior year, just two days away now. All summer Kelly had been talking about it, about how much fun it was going to be when they were the big-shot seniors, about classes and courses and college at the end of it, and about the potential of every boy in the class. She knew what college each of the better boys was headed for and what career, with what probable annual income. Jennifer was sick of listening and tuned it out.

It was almost eleven before Kelly finally left. Jennifer crawled into bed in the silent, dark apartment and sank gratefully into her daydreams: John's dark eyes intent upon her outside the tourney ground;

John's hand around hers as he led her to the oak tree and sat beside her; the awareness of his knee just within the folds of her skirt, not touching her, just communicating its warmth through the gown. And his voice, his surprisingly deep, rich voice singing love ballads. . . .

She was just fading into sleep when the apartment door opened downstairs and the muted but silence-breaking voices of her mother and the boyfriend woke Jennifer. There was hushed laughter, then a long silence, and then the closing of the door and Jackie's step on the stairs.

Jennifer's bedroom light blazed painfully in her eyes. "You awake, babe?" Jackie said brightly.

"I am now," Jennifer grumbled.

Jackie came in and sat with a bounce on the bed. She was as slim as Jennifer but in a more brittle, starved way. Her dark hair was dead straight and chopped off in geometric chic. Four-inch earrings swung beside her neck, and her shoulder pads were enormous under the plum silk cocktail dress.

"How was your day?" Jackie asked, lighting a cigarette and conscientiously blowing the smoke away from her daughter.

"Great," Jennifer muttered into the pillow. "It was fun."

"That's good, babe. Why you want to waste your weekends at that place is beyond me, but . . ." She made an airy motion with her cigarette, then eased her feet out of plum-colored spikes.

"Oh, man, these feet aren't as young as they used

to be. We didn't dance more than two, three hours at the most, with a lot of sitting and drinking in between, and I feel like I just ran the Boston Marathon in five-inch spikes. Hey, we went to that new place in Shakopee, there on Highway Five, you know? The Hawaiian Room. It was fantastic. You'd love it. They had this rock band, I forget their names, and this lead singer, young guy, cuter than hell. Wore white satin pants so tight you could see everything he owned, and I'm not talking car keys. You should have been there. You'd have loved it."

Jennifer opened one eye and fixed her mother with a steely gaze. "I'm too young and innocent to go to places like that, don't forget."

"Oh, I know that." Jackie made another sweeping motion with her cigarette, dropping ashes on the comforter. "But listen, you get yourself a date one of these Saturday nights, and we'll slap a ton of makeup on you and you can wear my black dress with the slit at the side. They'll never ID you. There were kids in there tonight who looked lots younger than you."

Jennifer grunted.

"Well, nighty-night, babe. See you very late in the morning. Oh no, you'll be working again, won't you?" Jackie got up with a final pat for Jennifer's shin and left.

Jennifer rolled to her other side, too roused by her mother's energy to go back to sleep now.

I almost liked her better when she was depressed, Jennifer thought. At least she was quieter back then, not always barging into my room and turning lights on when I'm trying to get to sleep. I should be glad the boat salesman didn't stay the night, I guess. I hate that. I really hate that. Mom's getting younger and sillier all the time. We're going to pass each other pretty soon, going in opposite directions as I get older.

It's having Michael out of the house that's making her so young. If they release him, what's going to happen then? God, just don't let them release Michael till after I leave for college.

No, that's not fair. Then Mom would be here all alone with him. She'd be terrified out of her mind.

Chris. Damn you, why did you run out on us? Mom and I loved you so much. We needed you to protect us from Michael, and you just turned tail and ran off. There wasn't anything wrong between you and Mom, and you know it. You just wanted to get out of here because you were afraid of Michael. Afraid he'd hold a knife to your throat and threaten to saw your head off like he did with Mom. And me.

I don't blame you for being scared, Chris. We all were. But you left us. We loved you and depended on you and you just left us.

Jennifer rolled over again, evading her thoughts. There was the other world waiting for her, for Lady Guinevere who lived in a castle outside the village and had a guardrobe full of lovely, long gowns. Her father was a famous knight who went to wars in the holy land and brought back treasures for his lovely daughter. And everyone loved the Lady Guinevere.

27

Knights and princes vowed to love her till they died, and they meant it, too.

But there was one, a king disguised as a wandering minstrel, who loved her more than all the others, and she loved him. They walked in a forest with sunlight slanting through the trees and tame fallow deer watching them pass. It was a world of safety and beauty and ease.

On this dream she finally wafted away.

❦ 5 ❦

"Nine o'clock, go home. Nine o'clock, go home." The town crier walked the lanes of the park, ringing his hand bell and crying his message.

John Turnbull stood beside the Ash Grove theater and watched the last of the crowd disappear down the avenue and out the three arched gates. The girl in the blue gown had passed the theater a few minutes before but hadn't noticed him standing in the shadows. It was just as well, he told himself.

The Ash Grove was a tiny theater in a small, wooded valley near the stock market. It was just a platform twelve feet square, with rows of plank-and-stump benches before it. It offered three shows a day, musicians and singers. Other theaters scattered through the fair specialized in Shakespeare, country dancing, jugglers and jesters and puppet shows, but the Ash Grove was for lovers of Renaissance music.

John had felt as tense and vibrant as one of his lute strings since that morning when he had looked down from the oak tree and seen the girl in the blue gown, dancing in her private joy. It was starting again, he thought.

Throughout the day he'd watched for the blue gown, seeing the girl from time to time in the distance, bending over a lost child or sharing her map of the fair with a confused visitor. He'd watched for several minutes at the jousting grounds while the maiden sat with the queen, smiled at the knights, and began her tour through the crowd with her tambourine trailing ribbons and flowers.

This was the girl, he knew. For this fair, the dark-haired dancing maid would be the one he sang his love ballads to. He said, as he always did, "I mustn't hurt her." And usually he didn't. Usually the girls he dreamed about and sang for were unaware of him or knew him only as the man who played and sang and watched them but seldom spoke.

With a practiced motion John flipped his cap onto his head without spilling any of the bills and coins he'd collected from the audience after his last set. He turned away from the now-darkened fair and followed an obscure path down into the ravine, across a tiny creek, and up again onto a flat, open area filled with trailers and motor homes.

John Turnbull's rig was an elderly Airstream, like a silver bullet, parked near the trees and unmowed weeds of the ravine. The location was quiet and private, though the mosquitoes were worse there than in the open.

Crossing the ravine from one century to another was still a small jolt for him, even after seven years of working fairs. The trailer city, the roar of generators, and the clash of rock music were jarring to him, especially in his present mood. He climbed into his trailer, put his lute away in its padded chamois bag, and took a quick shower in the cubicle that was bathroom and shower stall combined.

The cool comfort of jeans and T-shirt almost made up for the loss he felt when he peeled off the leather hose and jerkin. He made himself a late supper of cornflakes and a banana sliced lengthwise and spread with peanut butter. He was neither hungry before nor full afterward; his mind was on the girl in the blue gown.

From the next trailer, through open windows, came his neighbors' voices as loud and clear as though they were on stage. Jim and Helen Obermeier, retired, lived in Phoenix in the winter and spent the rest of the year traveling and working Renaissance fairs under the stage names of Barf and Gagg. Their comedy routine was loud and silly slapstick laced with ribald humor. She was exceedingly tall and thin; he was barely five feet tall and round as a basketball. Their routines were husband-wife squabbles.

Sometimes at night John wandered over to their trailer to pass the time, but tonight they were either working out a new routine or fighting in earnest. It was sometimes impossible to tell the difference from a trailer away.

But he didn't want to be alone tonight. If he lay in his dark trailer and followed his thoughts, he'd be in love before midnight, he knew. He recognized the glow already starting in him.

He took his flashlight and crossed the ravine again, climbing uphill past the Ash Grove and into the stock market. Horses and donkeys dozed on cocked legs within their rope pens. The donkey foal slept flat out, under her mother's belly, confident that she wouldn't be stepped on.

Around the fenced jousting grounds he went, toward a tiny, thatch-roofed hut beyond. Here in the open, the moonlight was sufficient. He snapped off the flashlight and saw then, in the altered night-light, the figure sitting outside the hut.

It was the square-built, black-bearded Scotsman who earlier had been playing the bagpipes. He had traded kilt for jeans, and bagpipe for a small bamboo flute, but he still wore the white ruffled shirt, open now to the waist.

Robert Colum sat on a stump, his back against the hut, one leg up and crossed over his knee. When he saw John coming toward him, he broke off the tune he'd been playing and tootled a lively chorus of "John Barleycorn," by way of greeting.

A black iron pot hung from a tripod before the hut. During the day the pot collected coins and bills from passing tourists who stopped to listen to his pipe tunes. Tonight the pot held ice cubes from the Quik-Trip Food and Fuel Mart on the highway, just a five-minute walk across the field. In the ice were set cans of beer, also from Quik-Trip.

"Partake," Robert said, motioning toward the pot of ice as John rolled a log-slice stump over beside Robert and sat down.

John opened a can and held it to his temple for the chill of it. "How was your day?" he asked.

Robert set the little bamboo flute over his ear like a pencil and picked up his own beer can from the grass. "Good first day," he said. "How about yourself?"

"Very profitable," John answered. They never asked or divulged exact amounts. The number of dollars the tourists dropped in a performer's cap or kettle was too clear an indication of worth. Comparisons were bound to be painful for the lesser-paid. And since earnings were reported to Internal Revenue only in proportion to the honesty of the earner, the entire subject was kept deliberately vague.

Robert said, "Did you try that fair in Arkansas you were talking about last year?"

"No, I was in Virginia. They've got a new one going out there in April and May, up in the mountains. Beautiful place. I've got the address if you want to give it a try. I did Florida and South Carolina over the winter, laid off in March, and then this new one in Virginia over the spring. Worked out just right."

"That wouldn't work for me," Robert said. "School."

"Oh, yes. I forgot you were local." John smiled through the darkness at the square, bearded face. He remembered now. Robert lived here in Minneapolis and went to college, just working this one fair rather than traveling from fair to fair as most of the performers did.

"What are you studying now, Middle Eastern religions, wasn't it?"

Robert laughed. "That was last year. This year I've taken up music philosophy. My old dad keeps sending me money to keep me from going home to Edinburgh and embarrassing the family, so here I'll stay till he runs out of brass or my brain explodes, whichever comes first."

John laughed.

"And how about you, John? Your life is still going on as it always has? You're a year older now than when we last met. Are you a year wiser?"

Coughing and snorting, John said, "Older, yes; no wiser atall, atall. I'm still looking with longing at the young lasses."

Grinning, Robert said, "You were drinking in that maiden in the blue dress this afternoon at the jousts, you dirty old lutanist. You've got to leave the young ones like that to me. I like them pure and innocent."

"No such thing as pure and innocent these days," John said. "They're all out there practicing safe sex and having protest marches for abortion clinics. They know more about it than I do, Robert. They scare hell out of me, these young girls."

He reached toward Robert and took the flute from

its nest above the Scotsman's ear. With a little exploratory fingering he picked out a tune, a sad little story-song about a girl who hanged her own true love in the dovecote when he refused to marry her and give their unborn child a name. But playing the flute prevented him from singing, and for him the words were always the important part of any song.

The two men talked on into the evening, slapping at mosquitoes on arms and necks, but preferring the night air to the stuffy, if bugless, hut behind them. Robert had built the hut himself, with materials provided by the fair commission, and had furnished it with the crude wood and pelt articles of a fifteenth-century Highland but-and-ben cottage.

"We could go inside," Robert said once.

But they didn't move. The night insects sang, and from time to time John or Robert hummed a bit or sang a few lines. Mostly they just sat enjoying the rest at the end of the day and the company of an easy friend.

Walking home after midnight, John was filled with the sense of well-being that came to him more and more frequently as his life ripened. He was in the right place, doing the right thing. This Renaissance fair in Minnesota, this September night, the day's work behind him and before him—all of it fitted John Turnbull as his leather breeches fit.

Even the girl in the blue gown—perfect for him to dream about this season. Unattainable, of course, but that was part of the perfection.

The next morning Jennifer looked for, and found, John the lute player up in the oak tree. For an hour she sat on the bench that girdled the tree and listened while he sat on that low branch, swinging one leg, strumming his lute, and pouring his soft, rich voice down over her. His cap sat open on the ground, and visitors dropped money into it, but neither of them noticed.

Today he wore black silken hose and pointed slippers of soft red leather. His blouse was huge, half red and half yellow, its fullness gathered by belt and ties at its neck and wrists. And today the lute wore a cord of red-and-gold woven silk.

As if they had conferred on the matter, Jennifer's gown was a dark, soft red with wide gold sleeves that fell almost to the ground when her arms were down.

Thanks to an early-morning session with Kelly, the hair above Jennifer's ears was braided, the two slim braids looped together at the back and decorated with daisies, white with gold centers. The mass of her hair fell to her shoulders as before, just crowned by the braid and its flowers.

When the hour and the songs were done, John dropped from the tree. "Thank you, Guinevere. I like having you with me when I sing. Will you come every morning and let me sing to you? You add to the music."

"No, I don't," she said, flushing and turning away. "But I'll come if you want me. I love to listen to you."

His eyes met hers; he seemed to shy away from something he saw there. But then he warmed and smiled and cocked his head to the side, studying her.

To keep him from leaving she said, "Do you live in this tree, or what?"

"Yes." He grinned. "At night I change into an owl. See my nest? Can you see it? Come over here and look straight up." She moved close and he rested his hands on her shoulders, so lightly she felt the warmth of his skin, not the touch of it.

"That's not an owl's nest, it's a robin's nest," she scoffed. "Already you're lying to me."

Too much! She'd said too much. That "already" would tell him that she expected . . . She half turned to face him and saw that he knew. He knew as well as she did that something, some future closeness, awaited them.

"Where do you eat lunch?" she asked just above a whisper.

He studied her face. "I'm too old for you, my lady Guinevere. You'll soon have pages and squires, even knights, at your feet. You don't want a tired old minstrel like me."

Jennifer drew back within herself, sensing his reluctance, remembering the pain of Chris's abandonment and fearing it again. But Guinevere stood erect and graceful and met his eyes with a bright, teasing look.

"You're quite right, my good man. I expect that if I turned on all my charm, I might attract the eye of Sir Lawrence the Lover."

John's carefully controlled expression shattered with laughter. Together they turned and walked along the lane toward the stock market, his hand lightly cupping Guinevere's elbow.

"My lady, you could attract his attention if you were wrapped to the eyeballs in a canvas tent. You could be stone-cold dead in the marketplace and Sir Lawrence would be making obscene suggestions to you and looking down the front of your gown."

"He does have an eye for the ladies," she said, falling easily into character.

"An eye, two hands, well, we won't go on. And now, fair maiden, I mustn't keep you from your duties."

"Supper then," Jennifer said quickly, needing to pin him down. "Where do you eat supper?"

The laughter left his eyes. Again he pondered her, and something in him drew away from her.

But after a silent moment he said, "Meet me at the Dragon's Breath Inn at six."

They separated at the edge of the stock market, John to do his morning stint on the Ash Grove stage, Jennifer to begin her wanderings in search of lost visitors to direct.

At noon she bought a mince pie from a shop called Simple Simon the Pieman. On the low roof above the pie shop sat a young man who, every few minutes, banged a pie tin with a wooden spoon and called out, "Get your hot, spiced mince pies right here, ladies and gentry, humble working folk and crooks and bastards and thieves and sheep farmers and the whole bloody lot of you. We're not proud. We'll serve anybody who buys our pies, but we're going to bite your coins to make sure they're real, so don't try anything."

To Jennifer he called down, "Come in and buy a pie, beautiful maiden. We make 'em from genuine hummingbird wings and rose petals, just for ladies like you. 'Course we have to mix in a little pigs' innards and oxtail to hold it all together. But you're going to love it. Ice-cold lemonade . . ."

"This fair certainly has a lot of guys on roofs and in trees," she called up to him.

"Safest place to be," he assured her with a wink. "If I was down there, all you girls would be grabbing at me."

At one-thirty a fair maiden riding sidesaddle on a small gray horse, the same pair Jennifer had seen yesterday, came trotting up to her and said, "Can you get over to the jousting stand? They're looking for maidens. They want to do a grand parade before the joust."

Jennifer picked up her skirts and half ran across the stock market to the jousting stand. Jerry, the announcer, waved her over and said, "You want to be in the parade? Grab yourself a mini and follow that guy over there."

Just behind her in the shade of the stock-pen grove stood three miniature horses, not a yard tall, peering at her from beneath long, bushy forelocks. Each wore a tiny gold bridle with a golden chain to lead him by. One was glossy black, one a bright red bay, and the smallest was black and white spotted.

Jennifer grabbed a chain and fell into line behind the man Jerry had indicated. The man wore a monk's robe and rode a mule. On to the jousting course they moved to the fanfare of the pair of trumpeters at the corners of the platform. The queen was on her throne, looking royally bored.

Around the course they walked, Jennifer leading the black mini by his golden chain. The little horse curvetted and pranced at the applause of the people along the rails. Ahead was the monk on his mule; behind her she caught glimpses of the other mini horses, the sidesaddle palfrey rider, and then the six knights in full armor on their high horses, bowing to the crowds and accepting their applause.

Back at the stand, the monk halted his mule to

40

bow before the queen and then moved on. Jennifer moved forward, did a curtsy learned unconsciously from the movies, and then led her tiny horse out of the arena.

The first of the jousts was announced: Sir James the Incredibly Good on his horse, Spotless, battling Sir Roger the Rotten, riding Meanbastard. Jennifer found a spot at the fence and watched, her tambourine forgotten at her side.

Sir James wore white; Sir Roger was all in black. The crowd hissed and booed with great energy as Roger galloped to the far end to take up his place. The trumpets blared, the horses charged. Jennifer had seen the knights' equipment at close range and knew that the lances they held were made of rubber. Still, she held her breath as the horses met at a full gallop, each on its side of the long barrier. Lances were thrust in passing. Sir Roger swerved but didn't fall. Both riders turned at the end of the course and came back at each other. Lances struck but no one fell. Back and forth they went, the crowd cheering and booing with equal enjoyment.

Finally the weary horses slowed to a stop across the barrier from each other, and Sir James stood in his stirrups to whomp Sir Roger over the helmet with his rubber lance. With great slow-motion drama, Sir Roger took the fall, rolling to the ground in a great racket of armor. Smiling, nodding, and bowing to the crowd, Sir James rode to the queen and received his prize, a small casket of fake jewels that he then strewed through the crowd.

Quickly Jennifer passed her tambourine, collecting donations while the crowd waited for the next pair of jousters.

Although she enjoyed the afternoon, Jennifer looked at her watch several times every hour and was at the Dragon's Breath Inn twenty minutes early.

It was at the far end of one of the narrow lanes, in an area Jennifer hadn't thoroughly explored. The inn was bigger than most of the shops, a square structure of timber and plaster and herringboned brick floors. The main room was square, with leaded-glass windows looking out in two directions. Jennifer found an empty table near a window and sat down to wait.

What am I doing here? she wondered suddenly. He's right. He's way too old for me to be messing around with. And I don't know anything about him, if he's married or what he does for a living or anything. And why is he interested in me instead of somebody his own age? He's more Mom's age than mine.

Then through the diamond-paned window she saw him walking down the lane, walking slowly as though he was reluctant to meet her. His head was down, his lute swinging at his side.

He looked up suddenly and stared directly through the window at her, his eyes finding her instantly. And it was there again in Jennifer: the shifting within her, the recognition of mate for mate.

7

Now it will start, Jennifer thought as John settled at the table and ordered their suppers. Now I'll start finding out about him and he'll ask all about me. . . .

But they talked instead about the food, listed on the menu as roasted dragon wings. They talked about the fair; Jennifer had seen more of it as a visitor than John had as a performer. She told him about the cobbler's shop in the middle lane where the shoemaker drew outlines of customers' feet, then in three hours made soft leather slippers with pointed toes that curled up and backward. With or without bells.

Jennifer waited through most of the meal for the expected questions: "Where do you live?" "Do you go to school?" The school question would tell him her age and so she dreaded it, but when the questions didn't come, she grew uneasy. Things she wanted to ask him about his life grew difficult to ask.

When the supper break was nearly over and nothing personal had yet been asked, she said, "Where do you live, John?"

"In that oak tree. I showed you my nest." His voice was matter-of-fact.

"Come on, get serious."

He looked at her, long and quietly. "I'd rather not, my lady. We minstrels have to be wary of seriousness. Too much of it can be fatal, you know."

He started to get up, but she held back. "You don't want to tell me where you live?" Her voice was rich with suppressed hurt. "You're married, aren't you?"

Sitting again, John took her hand and held it as lightly as if it were a sparrow. "No, my dear Lady Guinevere. I am not, nor ever have been, married. I am a wandering minstrel and that is no life for a woman or a family."

"No, but I mean in real life, John. Come on, tell me. Where do you live and what do you do, and are you married?"

"Come, my lady, let us sally forth. Others await our table." He nodded toward the line at the door.

Outside, he dropped an arm softly about her waist and steered her, not toward the center of the fair but past the end of the lane, around the corner of the inn, and down a footpath along the wooded ravine. They passed behind the Ash Grove stage and stopped.

"Over there," John said, pointing through the

44

trees. "That silver trailer. That's where I live. Alone. With neither chick nor child nor bonny bride. I told you I'm a wandering minstrel and I am. Canada in summer, here in the fall, Florida and the Carolinas in winter, Virginia in spring. Sometimes Renaissance fairs like this one, sometimes centennials or bluegrass festivals or what have you. I play banjo, too, and other things. It's my life. It's a good life for me."

Slowly Jennifer nodded. She heard what he was saying: Expect no long love from me. I'm just passing through your life, little girl. She twisted away from the painful point of his truth.

A voice in her head said, Go with him. Canada in summer, Virginia in the spring. . . .

His arm moved against her back. As she turned toward him, the tip of his finger lifted her chin. His kiss was so soft, it was barely a breath against her lips.

"And now, fair maiden, this poor minstrel must sing for his supper, and you must get on with your work. I shall hold you in my heart and praise you in my songs."

The next day, Labor Day, was oppressively hot even at eight in the morning when the fair gates opened. Nonvirgins passed through the virgin gate just for the refreshment of the splash of water from the guard's bucket.

Once again Jennifer sat beneath the minstrel's oak tree while he sang to her and for the crowd. "In a

45

field by the river, my love and I did stand, And on my leaning shoulder she laid her snow-white hand. She bid me take love easy, as the grass grows on the weirs; But I was young and foolish, and now am full of tears."

While she listened and drank in the look of him, Guinevere knew he loved her. She sat gracefully, more gracefully than Jennifer Dean; she moved with limpid fluidity, laying a snow-white hand on the minstrel's foot as it swung from the tree limb.

Visitors wandered past, moving more slowly today in the heat. In clumps of two or three, they stopped and stood at a little distance from Guinevere and the minstrel, absorbing the music and its mood. Money landed discreetly in the cap.

Today Guinevere followed John Lutanist's lead. No talk of twentieth-century reality; no talk at all, only the music and the make-believe world it wove about them.

At the end of the hour, it was she who walked away first. His song followed, still holding her to him: "She stepped away from me and went through the fair, And fondly I watched her move here and move there. And then she went homeward with one star awake, As the swan in the evening moves over the lake. . . . And I smiled as she passed with her goods and her gear, And that was the last that I saw of my dear."

All day the air lay like a smothering blanket over the fair. The lanes and the grassy avenue were crowded with visitors, but all moved in slow motion and most carried cans of soft drinks or dripping ice-cream bars or slush cones.

Today Jennifer wore the third and last of the gowns issued to her by the fair. This was, luckily, the coolest of the three, a gauzy, white peasant dress sprigged with tiny blue forget-me-nots and tied with blue ribbons under the bodice. The skirt rode on a froth of petticoats. The dress had come accompanied by a headband that trailed blue ribbons and tiny blue and white flowers. Against the dark cloud of her hair, the effect was lovely.

After lunch, as she was making her way through the stock market toward the jousts, Jennifer noticed a man standing in an oddly tense pose under the trees near the horse pens. He was middle-aged, heavy, and bald, with a painful-looking sunburn on his head and ears.

He stood motionless, his hands raised in front of him. She went to him and said, "Excuse me, are you all right?"

He turned frightened eyes toward her and opened his mouth but said nothing.

"Can you walk?" she asked abruptly. The first-aid building was just down the lane. Taking his arm, she eased him toward it. A step, another step. He leaned toward her until most of his weight was against her. Another step and another, and they were inside the building.

The nurse met them at the door, eased the man down onto her cot, and spoke into a tiny hand phone that hung from her belt.

"Heart attack," she murmured to Jennifer. "Don't worry. The paramedics are just outside the fairgrounds. They'll be here in two minutes. A day like this always takes its toll. Just relax now, sir. You're going to be fine as frog's hair. A little ride in our private limousine, and you'll be fine."

Jennifer knelt beside the cot and held his hand. "Do you have someone here with you? Family?"

The man was breathing painfully now. "My daughter, grandkids. Red hair. Find them. . . ."

The nurse pried his hand from Jennifer's and motioned with her head toward the door. "Go and see if you can find them," she said. She began loosening the man's shirt and belt.

Jennifer ran from the room, strung with tension. Find them? How? Who? She didn't even have his name.

Back to the stock market she ran, looking for anyone with red hair. And there they were, a young woman and two small redheaded children. The woman was looking at her watch and studying the crowd, searching for a face. The children, their backs to her, were holding out swatches of grass to the donkey foal.

With the briefest possible introduction and explanation, Jennifer led the family to the first-aid building and left them. The paramedics were there, working over the man with their profession's unique blend of speed and reassurance.

Through the long, sweaty afternoon, Jennifer thought about the man, wondered if he was alive.

She hoped so; he had given her a moment of excitement and importance and she wished him well.

By suppertime the sky had gone from a brassy yellow haze to dark and lowering clouds. The visitors gazed upward, looked at each other, and began moving toward the gates and their waiting cars.

When Jennifer reported for duty at the jousting stand a little before eight, Jerry said, "I don't know if we'll get through this session before the thunder boomers hit, but we'll give it a try, anyhow. Let's skip the parade and just call the first joust. Hey, Guinevere, you want to be the prize tonight?"

"Sure. Why not?" She had no idea what that involved, but she was too wilted and sweaty to care. In another few minutes, the storm would break and they could all go home, anyway.

The queen shifted her crown and muttered, "My head's so sweaty I can't keep this thing up. And my arthritis is killing me. Let's call it off and go home, Jerry."

"Shut up and reign," he said. He flipped on his mike and announced, "Ladies, gentlemen, and peasants, we're going to get started a little early tonight because the rain gods are about to show us their displeasure. First contest tonight is between Sir Godfrey the Stupid and Sir Harold the Huge. Let's give 'em a big hand here, folks."

Applause applause.

"And to make it more exciting, the winner of this joust may claim the hand of the lovely and virginal

Lady Guinevere, sitting right over here at the feet of her queen."

Jennifer rose and curtsied to the crowd.

The knights rode up and bowed to their queen, then moved their horses over to Jennifer for a close inspection of their prize. The crowd laughed and clapped as Sir Godfrey tried to lift her skirt for a peek.

Sir Godfrey the Stupid did everything wrong. He rode on the wrong side of the barrier, bringing his horse into a collision course with Sir Harold's horse, Unlucky. Godfrey got his reins tangled in his lance, dropped the lance and had to dismount to pick it up, and when the two knights finally engaged in combat, Godfrey struck with the wrong end of the rubber lance.

Just as the first raindrops fell, Jerry announced, "Honors to Sir Harold the Huge, who wins the hand of the fair Lady Guinevere. That's all for tonight, folks. Run like hell!"

He grabbed the queen by the hand, and they disappeared into the sheeting rain. Jennifer stood at the edge of the platform, uncertain whether to stay under the canopy or to make a run for her car.

Suddenly Sir Harold the Huge galloped up in a spray of mud and rain and grabbed her around the waist with one arm. Squealing, she clung to his back and fought for balance astride the horse. Her skirt rode up her legs; her hair plastered against her face, blinding her.

"Help! Where are you taking me?" she screeched.

And then the rain ceased to strike her, and the horse jolted to a stop. Wiping the hair from her eyes, Jennifer looked around. They were inside the long, low barn at the back of the stock market. The place was crowded with steaming horses and laughing, dripping people.

A hand rested softly on her foot. Guinevere looked down into the black-bright eyes of John Lutanist. All else receded from her sight and hearing; there was only him.

A voice in her ear bellowed, "Unhand that maiden's foot, you scoundrel. I won her fair and square. She's mine." Harold the Huge jabbed at John's vest with his rubber lance.

"But her heart belongs to me," John said in his deep, soft singing voice. His eyes held Guinevere's.

He lifted his arms and she slid down into them, her wet skirts falling about her legs. She shivered, more from tension than from chill, but he held her close to warm her with his body.

The shifting sensation deep inside her became more acute. If they'd been alone, she would have pressed herself full length against him and wanted more than that.

"Robert," he called as he eased away from her, "have you got something for this girl?"

The Scottish piper came through the crowd bearing a sheepskin rug from his hut. He'd been dispensing towels and blankets from his meager store in the hut just beyond the barn.

Wrapping the sheepskin around her shoulders,

John led her to a quiet corner and settled her on a bale of hay at the base of a mountain of bales.

"Stay here," he said. "I think they've got a coffee machine going over on the other side. I'll bring you something hot to drink."

"No. Stay with me." She opened her arms and offered him the warmth within.

They sat close together in the sheepskin, saying nothing, savoring the touch of body against body.

8

The storm lasted less than an hour, but by the time it was finished, the barn full of people had become a party. The knights' horses were settled in their stalls along one long side of the barn, and a coffee machine had been set up on a tack trunk. Robert made a run to the Quik-Trip for beer and ice and munchies, while someone else produced a case of canned pop. Bottles of hard liquor appeared and were passed.

Some of the people who had ducked into the barn for shelter were visitors; some were fair workers, knights, concessionaires. Jennifer recognized the man who ran the elephant ride and the girl who rode the gray palfrey sidesaddle.

Robert came and sat beside John and Jennifer on the hay pile, watching them and smiling somewhere deep in his eyes. To Jennifer he said, "This man will break your heart, you know." And to John he said, "She's a genuine beauty, my friend. Better than you deserve, and she'll break your heart. I guarantee it."

Sir Harold the Huge struggled out of his armor and spent the evening in long underwear bottoms and a T-shirt, stomping about the barn and shouting that the miserable minstrel had stolen his prize virgin.

"I won her fair and square," he bellowed to anyone who would listen. "He can't have her. He has to give her back to me."

Nested against John, wrapped with him in the sheepskin, Jennifer felt the scene impressing itself so deeply in her that it would always be there. Fifty years from now, she knew, she would close her eyes and see this barn and these people; she would feel again what she felt now for the man beside her. And no other loves, no matter how sensible they might be, would ever quite match the intensity of the anticipation that strummed between her and John.

Would it be tonight? she wondered. Would he take her back to his silver trailer and bed her there? When it happens to me, she swore silently, it's going to be for love and permanence—and nothing less than that.

Jennifer felt confident that, for her, that ultimate intimacy would be possible only with a man mature enough to be depended upon, a man who loved her totally and would never leave her. Otherwise the risk would be too great. Self-preservation would keep her from opening herself to such wounds as Chris had inflicted. Or her father.

She couldn't love without security; that was the one positive in her slowly growing knowledge of Jennifer Dean.

But now she sat in this dim and steamy barn, huddled in a sheepskin with a man she knew nothing about, a man far older than herself who lived in a trailer at a Renaissance fair and avoided talking about himself. Safe? Dependable? Even as she scoffed at herself, she couldn't deny the instinct that told her this was her mate.

The night grew late. Jennifer wondered whether her mother was home yet. Probably not. Her company's annual picnic was today, and Jennifer knew from previous years that the party seldom broke up before dawn.

John took her arm and said simply, "Come."

She followed him through the barn and out into the night. Near the door they passed Robert, who looked solemnly at the two of them, then shook his head in a slow warning to John.

"What was that for?" Jennifer asked him as they picked their way across the muddy ground by the jousting course.

"He was warning me," John said. "Robert enjoys a pessimistic outlook. He assumes I'm going to defile your innocence and that we'll both suffer for it afterward."

"Are you?"

He walked on at a steady pace. "No, I'm not. I'm going to take you to your car and bid you goodnight."

She stopped and turned to him. They were near their oak tree now.

"Why?" she said.

"Why?"

"Yes. Why are you taking me to my car instead of your trailer?"

He looked at her for a silent eternity, then brushed a strand of hair from her forehead with his fingertips. "Because, my lovely Lady Guinevere, dreams are dreams and reality is fatal to them. I want my dreams of you, and you want your dreams of me, and if we get too close, we'll start seeing through one another."

There was no answer. Frustrated and furious, Jennifer turned and ran down the long avenue toward the gates. Veering sharply, she detoured through the virgin gate in a gesture of spite. She halted and turned and saw the black shape of him watching from beside the tree.

"Fool. Damned fool," John muttered as he climbed the muddy creek bank toward his trailer. "She was offering; all I had to do was take. Her responsibility, not mine."

Yet he knew he had been right. He showered and settled on his bed at the end of the trailer. He propped pillows behind him and lay the lute across his lap for company. In the dark he plucked the strings, making soft, unmusical sounds until a melody came out of them.

It was a good melody, a new one. Excitement grew in him. It had been years now since a song had seeded itself in his mind and sprouted, not since the last time he'd loved. . . .

First the tune fitted itself together, and then the words began to build, one on another until they made a song.

"She was a dream and a vision of mine, Born from my loneliness, born from my need. She was my dream and a vision divine. Till I kissed her and took her to me.

"Till I kissed her and took her to me, to me, Till I kissed her and took her to me.

"She was a woman then, woman of mine, With a voice and a touch and a need of her own. She was a woman then, less than divine, And the dream I had loved, of her, oh, it was flown.

"For I kissed her and took her to me, to me, For I kissed her and took her to me."

9

School was a time-warp unreality for Lady Guinevere. She had to become Jennifer again, and she didn't want to. She wanted to live forever at the fair, listening to love ballads pouring down on her from the oak tree on the village green.

Instead, she listened to Kelly Green's shrill chatter every morning in the Toyota on the way to school and every afternoon on the way home. She learned her class schedule and began the year's marathon of studying chapters and writing assignments, but more than half of her was Guinevere at the fair.

And John. She sketched his face in light pencil on the back pages of her spiral notebooks. She spent two study periods in the school library reading about lutes and other medieval instruments. After the first Glee Club practice, she asked the vocal music teacher for books of early Renaissance folk music. For a research project, she explained. But it was the only way she could touch John during the school week.

On Thursday afternoon Kelly stayed late for Camera Club, which she'd joined because it had the best boy-girl ratio of any of the special-interest school clubs. Free of Kelly, Jennifer drove south out of town to the Quik-Trip near the fair.

She pulled in and filled her gas tank as slowly as possible. Not much hope . . . but there was always a chance. . . . Robert could come over to the station for ice or beer or something and see her there. She'd just happened to stop for gas, out this way giving somebody a ride home from school maybe. And Robert would say, "Come on over to the hut." And she'd go, and John would wander over. . . .

A car honked. Jennifer woke to the fact that she'd been standing for some time with the gas pump hose in her hand, and that three cars were lined up waiting for her place at the pumps.

She paid for her gas and drove to the edge of the concrete apron, where she could see the tops of the fair buildings across the field. The line of trees delineated the ravine; the sun glinted from the tops of trailers and motor homes lining the ravine.

John was over there. Just across that field. A track that was almost a road led from the Quik-Trip across the dried grass of the field to the performers' camp.

All I have to do is drive over there, she thought. Just turn down that track and drive over there and cruise around till I see him. Five o'clock on a Thursday afternoon; what would he be doing? What does he do all week when the fair's not on? I don't even know that about him. I don't know thing one about him, but I'm in love with him. Doesn't make sense. Why couldn't I feel this way about Dennis?

Dennis was her lab partner in physics, and he liked her. He smiled with genuine pleasure when he saw her, and his eyes followed her covertly. He was taller than Jennifer, and pleasant looking, and one of the smartest in the class. A logical senior-year boyfriend. But . . .

But he wasn't John Turnbull, John Lutanist, John the warm-eyed wandering minstrel whose look heated Jennifer's blood.

In John there was a strength and sureness that no eighteen-year-old boy could possess. He was safe to lean against. To love.

As she sat behind the wheel of the Toyota and stared across the field, her courage failed her. She couldn't go to him when she wasn't sure he wanted her. She put the little car in gear, circled the dumpsters, and headed home.

Jackie Dean was in the little room off the living room, which served as her at-home office. Here she spent long hours studying investment portfolios, Dow Jones graphs, and tax-exempt-interest charts. In the evenings she called on her clients, mostly middle-income families and career women. She planned their investments for them, advising government bonds or sector funds or perhaps safe CDs and money markets.

When Jennifer came in, she found her mother at the computer desk staring absently at a screen full of clients' names. Jackie raised a hand in wordless greeting.

"Hey, guess what," she called as Jennifer turned toward the kitchen. "Chris called. He broke up with that fluffhead he was going with."

Jennifer turned. "So?"

"So we're going out tomorrow night."

Jennifer nodded. It was all going to start again, her mother and Chris . . . and herself? If Chris was in the house again, was she going to be half in love with her own stepfather all over again? Was he going to run out on them again the minute things got rough?

She moved up the stairs placidly. No, Chris wasn't important anymore. He was Jackie's business, no longer a central part of Jennifer's happiness.

Friday afternoon. As they had been for the last year, Jennifer's classes were scheduled so that she had the last period free on Friday. Jackie's little BMW pulled into the school's drive just as Jennifer came out, blinking, into the sun. It was an hour's drive to Parkhurst, the detention facility where Michael lived.

Friday afternoon: family conference time.

Michael and Dr. Prudholm were already in the small gray-and-rose room used for family conferences. The doctor smiled, held the door open for

Jennifer and Jackie, and motioned to their usual chairs.

Dr. Prudholm was a small woman in her sixties, with a golfer's leathery skin and a mannish haircut. Her voice was clear, direct, matter-of-fact.

"Michael's had an excellent week," she said by way of greeting.

Jackie gave her son a quick hug and kiss; Jennifer smiled at him but hung back. She hated these conferences. She hated her brother, although she didn't allow those words to form in her mind.

He was a strikingly handsome young man, tall and well built, with Jennifer's soft dark hair and large hazel eyes under gracefully shaped brows. He wore a green polo shirt and slim-fitting sport slacks. A big brother any girl would treasure. Any girl who hadn't seen the rage, the savagery twisting the handsome face into a nightmare fright mask.

He had been her big brother, her teacher, her superior in their early years, like any big brother. Sometimes he pushed her too hard and made her fall, or twisted the skin of her arm in a painful pinch to make her cry. But all big brothers did that, didn't they? It was her fault, for bothering him.

Then one summer day at White Bear Lake, Michael caught a frog and brought it over to the place on the beach where Jackie had been inflating water toys with a small foot pump. When Jackie went back to the car to get something, Michael held Jennifer's attention riveted in horror as he jammed the pump's nozzle into the rear of the frog and with three savage pumps exploded the creature.

After that Jennifer shrank from Michael's attention. She avoided him as much as possible. When Petey, the parakeet, drowned by falling headfirst into a glass of water, Jennifer hid her eyes from the sight of Michael parading through the apartment holding glass and dead bird over his head. But she didn't tattle on him. She didn't say to her mother, "Michael killed Petey. I know he did."

It was about the time Jackie married Chris, when Jennifer was eleven and Michael fourteen, that her brother's violence became obvious to the whole family. He had gotten up from the supper table one night and started toward the door. Jackie asked where he was going.

"Out."

"Where and with whom?" she insisted.

"None of your damn business. You don't own me." He stood near the kitchen counter, rigid with sudden tension. Jennifer, seeing the flare of rage in his eyes, shrank in her chair.

Chris started to rise. "You listen here, young man. You don't talk to your mother that way. You're not going anywhere tonight. You . . ."

Suddenly the bread knife was in Michael's hand. He lunged for Jackie and held her against him, the knife pressing into her throat.

He was tall for fourteen, taller than his mother, and much stronger. Jackie made a faint whimpering cry and sagged against the table.

"No one is the boss of me," Michael screamed. He dropped his mother and slammed out the door, still carrying the knife.

When he came home several hours later, nothing was said about the attack, by anyone in the family. Michael had taken over position of alpha wolf in their family pack, and no one challenged him.

It was two years later when the second explosion came, two years in which an armed truce existed in the household. No one pushed Michael, so no one was threatened by him.

Then Kelly Green moved to the complex, spotted Michael, and began hanging around in the guise of Jennifer's friend. The two girls were in Jennifer's room one night trying on shirts, looking for interesting layering combinations, when Michael pushed open the door and stood there staring at Kelly in her bra.

"Get out," Jennifer yelled at him. Kelly squealed and wrapped something around her, but not without a gleam of excitement in her eyes.

He came into the room, reached calmly for Kelly's breast, and mashed it as though he were crunching a beer can. The look was in his eyes—rage and something else, something worse.

Jennifer shouted, "Chris, get him out of here." She got between Michael and Kelly, whose mouth was squared open in a cry of surprise and pain, and pushed against her brother with all her strength.

He grabbed her. There was a click, and a knife

point dug into the side of Jennifer's neck. She went faint with terror.

No one spoke.

From the bedroom door Chris said, "What's going on in here?"

Jennifer was flung against the bed; Michael pounded out of the room, out of the apartment, slamming the door behind him.

After that came months of sessions with school counselors and family counselors. Michael went willingly enough. He seemed to enjoy talking about himself and being the center of concern and attention. He became adept at feeding back to the psychologists the answers they wanted from him.

But the rage episodes continued and grew more frequent. Once he broke every breakable dish in the kitchen, cutting himself superficially on the arm with a jagged curve of broken glass. Once when Jackie ignored a question he was asking, while she talked to a client on the phone, Michael ripped the phone cord from the wall and wrapped it around her throat, pulling it just tight enough to make her eyes bulge and her face turn dark red, before he let her go. "You answer me when I talk to you," he told her through clenched teeth.

When Chris moved out, things seemed to get better. Michael was the unchallenged alpha wolf, with Jackie and Jennifer cowed by his rages. Then one of his teachers corrected him in class for getting out of his seat without permission and pacing across the back of the room. Michael flung himself toward the teacher, a man of Michael's own size and strength. It took five students to pull his hands from the teacher's throat.

Michael had been in Parkhurst since that day. Three years now, Jennifer thought, three years of visits to this place and family conferences.

There had been in-depth analyses and group sessions and, this past year, hormone treatments that did seem to calm him temporarily.

"Jennifer?" Dr. Prudholm was saying.

"What? I'm sorry, I wasn't listening."

Dr. Prudholm used her cold, straight smile to diminish Jennifer. "Family conferences don't work unless the whole family participates, do they, dear?"

"Sorry," Jennifer muttered.

"We were discussing the fact that Michael will be twenty-one in just a few weeks, and that's our maximum age limit here at Parkhurst, you know. We've been reviewing his progress at our staff meetings, and we're all agreed that Michael is ready to come home now. How do you feel about that, Jennifer? Wouldn't it be nice to have your brother back home?"

Nice? *Nice?*

Jennifer stared at Dr. Prudholm, then at her mother, whose face was stiff and white around the mouth.

"Michael has responded beautifully to the hormone treatments, and we see no reason why he shouldn't be perfectly able to get on with his life

66

now, get into college. Of course he'll have some adjustments to make. He understands that, don't you, Michael?"

"Sure." He smiled his bland, blank-eyed smile at the woman who could give him his freedom. Then, for a split second those eyes met Jennifer's, and she knew. The rage was still there, banked and hidden until he was free of the doctors and the institution.

It was still there.

Dr. Prudholm went on. "Nothing has been decided definitely yet. The alternative would be to transfer Michael to Saint Cloud, which is an adult facility, as you know. Our director will be talking with Michael in depth this week, and there'll be another staffing Thursday. The final decision will be made then, but we feel optimistic, don't we, Michael?"

He nodded and smiled his careful smile.

"Well?" Dr. Prudholm prompted, seeking thanks for her gift to Michael's family.

"Wonderful," Jackie said faintly.

Jennifer nodded. It was the most she could bring herself to do.

On the ride home, she tuned out her mother's voice, talking about fixing up a room for Michael. Every atom of her was pulling toward the Renaissance fair.

Sir Roger the Rotten won the hand of the fair Lady Guinevere in the last joust of Saturday night's program.

"Help, save me," Guinevere cried piteously to the crowd along the fence as Sir Roger carried her away on the front of his saddle.

"Heh, heh, heh, me proud beauty," Roger crowed loudly. "I shall have my way with ye tonight."

They galloped off the jousting course and down the slope toward the barn. It was a few minutes past nine. The town crier had come around already, calling, "Nine o'clock, go home." The crowd of visitors melted away toward the grass avenue and the entrance gates.

Now is the best time, Guinevere thought. The strangers are all gone, and John might . . . He was there in the gathering dark, his white blouse standing out against the night, his lute swinging at his side.

Roger loosed his hold around her waist so that she settled to the ground beside John. Then he steered Meanbastard into the barn, where they both would get out of costume.

Guinevere smoothed the red-and-gold gown down over her rear and faced John in hopeful silence. They were both free now. If he wanted to be with her, this was the time.

He took her hand and held it, but said nothing. The clasped hands swung between them as though moved by the forces of attraction and evasion.

"I was going to Robert's," he said.

Guinevere waited. Was it an invitation or not?

Abruptly he turned toward the Scotsman's hut and led Guinevere there. Robert met them at the door and ushered them in with no sign of surprise on his face.

We are a couple, Guinevere thought.

There was an early autumn chill in the air that night. In the small stone fireplace at the kitchen end of the hut, a fire burned. Robert poured red wine into three earthenware mugs, then added cinnamon and orange slices from the crude table near the fire. Finally he stirred the mixtures with a narrow iron rod that he took from the fire, glowing red.

"Hot mulled wine," he pronounced. "One of life's luxuries."

The hut was a single room the size of Jennifer's bedroom. Rough chairs made of wood slabs and

69

leather thongs flanked the fireplace. The dirt floor was carpeted with skeepskins; grass grew along the edges near the walls. The four small windows seemed to be made of parchment instead of glass.

Along the wall opposite the fireplace was a low bed made of lashed branches and a pair of huge feather-beds, comforters stacked for sleeping between.

"Do you know this one then?" Robert said, picking up a small lap-held harp and strumming it. He sat in one of the two fireside chairs. John motioned Guinevere toward the other chair while he himself sat on the floor, leaning against her leg with his lute in playing position.

With a sharply strummed chord from the lap harp, Robert sang, "Never shove a granny off a bus, never shove a granny off a bus, Never shove a granny, 'cause she's your mammy's mammy, oh . . . never shove a granny off a bus."

The three of them laughed together and welded a friendship. The hot mulled wine was delicious. Jennifer drained her mug and hoped for more, but wouldn't interrupt the music for it.

Robert sang, and John picked up the melodies and joined in on choruses, while Guinevere stored the moment in her heart.

"Thou art the music of my heart, Harp of joy, o cruit mo chridh, Moon of guidance by night, Strength and light thou art to me."

"'An Eriskay Love Lilt,' that's called," Robert said. "From *Songs of the Hebrides*."

"More, please," Guinevere whispered.

Robert sang the next chorus alone, while John's hand reached up for hers and held it, squeezing lightly.

"When I'm lonely, dear white heart, Black the night or wild the sea, By love's light my foot finds the old pathway to thee. Vair me o, ro van o, Vair me o, ro van ee, Vair me o, ru o ho, Sad am I without thee."

The lovely, haunting melody lay on the air in the hut. Guinevere wanted to cry for the poignancy of the moment.

Robert said, "The chorus is in Gaelic. I'd translate, but it'd lose something if I tried."

Later they laid aside their instruments and mulled another round of wine. As Robert handed Guinevere her mug, he said, "Now then, lass, tell me about yourself. Are you in school?"

"High school. Senior this year."

She didn't want to revert to Jennifer and bring her life into the hut. It didn't belong here. But as Robert asked the get-acquainted questions, she was conscious of John, listening, learning about her. Robert was asking what John himself should have asked.

"How about you?" she asked of Robert, cutting John out.

"I am a bum, essentially." The broad, red face split into a grin that widened his beard. "I am a professional student. I love being a student, and I intend to go on as long as I can get away with it. Much more pleasant than taking on the real world."

"Are you really from Scotland, or is that a fake accent?"

"What accent? You're the ones who talk funny. No, I'm from Edinburgh and I'll go back there when I have to, but I like to think of myself as a citizen of the world. Now our John here, he's a citizen of the world, for sure."

She looked down at the top of John's head, the beak of his nose, the rims of his ears. She loved him.

"Where were you born?" she asked him.

"Cape Breton, South Africa." He strummed a chord.

"South Africa? Really? I thought you sounded British." She felt gauche and very young. South Africa!

"My family was English," he went on in a soft, absentminded sort of voice, as though he'd told the story too many times. "My dad was in the service, stationed down there. I left when I was fifteen. Ran away from home and joined a band, taught myself to play backup guitar and sing a little. We went all over South Africa and Australia before we broke up. I kept on going, though, with other bands and then on my own. New Guinea, Canada, the States."

"You never got married? Honestly?"

He shook his head against her knee.

Robert shifted to the bed and stretched out on the feather mattresses, sinking almost out of sight but holding aloft his wine mug.

"I'm not ever going to marry, either. See now, John, you've become my role model in life. I'll be a wandering minstrel when I've finished being a bum student. No family to tie me down, no kiddies and no responsibilities. A totally selfish life, that's for me."

They laughed.

Jennifer said, "But you need someone to love you, Robert. Everybody needs that. Do you want to grow old alone?"

"Hah. I never said alone, did I? There are always ladies for the loving. . . ."

"And the leaving?"

John sat silently, watching the two of them.

"Of course for the leaving," Robert insisted. "What we call love is built to self-destruct. By its very nature, it's self-limiting, girl. When it starts it's all very intense, very strong and real, and you know, you *know* it's going to last forever. But it changes as the people change. Something of it might last, but in a different form, not that first magnificent passion. So I say, enjoy the early stage of the thing and then move on to a new love and another exciting early stage."

John said, "It's part of nature's design for the survival of the species, don't you think? We have some sensory device in us, like the instinct that guides birds when they migrate. Something in us makes us respond to one person, draws us to that person until we've mated and reproduced, and that's all nature wanted from us. The bond starts to dissolve and we're free to go, maybe find other mates and reproduce again."

Jennifer said, "But what about homes and families

and permanence?" It was a cry from her heart, but the words came out normally.

"That's part of the natural instinct, too," Robert said. "Shelter and nurture for the young of the species until they can survive on their own. It was simpler in caveman days, but the way we live, it comes down to paying rent and buying food and paying child support. If we were forest creatures, the male would drag home carcasses of his kill for the cubs in the den, and that would be his part in it.

"Have you ever held a puppy and had it lick you under the chin? They all do that, you know. In the wild, dogs and wolves have a little spot under the chin that triggers a vomiting reflex. A she-wolf with weanling cubs will go out and kill and eat, then come home and the cubs will lick her under her chin to make her vomit. They can digest the food in that form, you see, whereas they couldn't digest it raw."

"Thank you for sharing that lovely story," Jennifer said sourly, and they all laughed.

John said, "It's true. Nature rules our lives even as twentieth-century humans. We search for mates, and we know them when we find them. By instinct, not by practicality or being sensible. By instinct."

"You're taking me back to my car, again, aren't you?" Jennifer said as he walked her across the midnight black stock market.

"Yes." He said it sadly, firmly.

She stopped and turned to him. "I know what you meant about finding a mate instinctively."

He looked at her silently, running his two hands up and down her arms. "Yes," he said again.

"But you're taking me to my car."

"We live in a civilized world, lovely Jennifer. There are repercussions. Actions create situations."

"Because you're older than me? I don't care about that. I feel"—she pulled in a long breath—"I feel that you are my natural mate."

He drew her to him gently, gently, and kissed her hair, her forehead, her nose. She moved and captured him then, and the kiss was long and deep.

"Get out of here," he said at last.

She stood unmoving until he turned away himself and ran off into the dark lane.

𝕴𝕴

The weekdays slowed to a crawling pace for Jennifer. Was it only Tuesday? How could it be only Wednesday? When she tried to concentrate on her schoolwork, it slipped sideways from her mind. Only her strongest efforts and constant reminders of the gradepoint average she would need for college entrance kept her on her toes.

College. It seemed less vital to her now, a childhood dream that she'd outgrown. The nebulous vision of herself as a historian, anthropologist, or teacher was growing hazy, a remembered dream that fades on waking.

More and more she thought of herself living in a trailer in Canada in summer, the Carolinas in spring; living in a world of music and make-believe jousts, where everyone went home happy when the town crier told them to go. A lifetime of listening to John's love ballads and seeing the love in his eyes for her; a lifetime of happiness. How could four years of college and a boring job compare with flowing gowns and lute music and John?

When she got home from school on Thursday, she found her mother lying on the sofa with a wet washcloth over her eyes.

"What's the matter? Are you sick?"

"No. Headache," Jackie said in a muffled voice.

And Jennifer knew. She dropped her books on the end table and sat down to stare, dismayed, at Jackie. Jackie turned her head, opened one eye, and looked at her.

"Dr. Prudholm called this afternoon."

Jennifer sighed. "They're releasing him, aren't they? You haven't had those headaches since Michael left. When?"

"Sunday," Jackie said dully. "She called to tell us not to bother to come for our family session tomorrow. They're releasing him Sunday, which is his twenty-first birthday. Don't forget to get him something, by the way. Take a twenty from my purse and get him a shirt or whatever, okay? And a funny card. I can pick up a cake at the Supervalue Saturday."

Jennifer sighed. "Mom, be honest. You really don't want Michael back here, do you?"

Jackie unfolded the washcloth so that it covered her whole face, not just her eyes. "Of course I want him here. He's my son and I love him."

"You're lying through your teeth, Mom. Also

77

through your washcloth. You're still scared of him, and I am, too. I don't think all those years of therapy and treatments did a damn thing for him. He's a mean, cruel person, brother or no brother, and he still scares me, even just being in the conference room with him and Dr. Prudholm."

"Oh, no, I think you're wrong. I think he's better." Jackie's voice, muffled by the cloth, lacked conviction.

"Maybe he won't want to stay here," Jennifer said brightly. "He'll be twenty-one. He'll probably go right out and get a job and an apartment of his own, and. . . ," she faltered.

Sighing, Jackie sat up. "Oh, yes. He's going to waltz right out of that mental institution and get himself hired, with his record for violent behavior. Yes, I have a clear vision of that, kiddo."

"More likely he'll be on the streets selling drugs or something," Jennifer said darkly. "And you know what, I don't even care. That's a terrible thing to say, but it's true. All I want is to never have to see him again in my life."

She stopped when she saw the tears, black with mascara, on her mother's cheeks.

"He's my *son*. I have to love him. I do love him. I love that little, fat, smiling baby boy that I used to play with for hours, Jennie. He was such a miracle for your father and me. You were, too, just as much as Michael in your own way. But that first baby . . . there's just nothing like it in your whole life. A human being that came out of my body. It just blew me away. I'd lie down on the floor and stand him on my stomach, lean him against my legs, you know, and he'd dance back and forth with those tiny little feet in my gut, hanging onto my fingers for balance, and just grinning and grinning."

Jennifer ached for her mother.

In a low voice Jackie said, "The worst of it is, well, the timing stinks. Chris and I had such a good time the other night. The old magic is still there, for both of us. I think he'd come back, but . . ."

"What, you mean you might marry him again? Did he say anything?"

"Oh, not anything definite, just a lot of reminiscing about our good old days together, stuff like that. He said that fluffhead he was going with was driving him nuts and making him realize how wonderful I was."

John was better, Jennifer thought. He never married because true love hadn't come along for him yet. Till now. But he wouldn't go back and forth, marrying and divorcing and remarrying, like Chris. John was strong enough to know his own mind and do what was right. With her he was holding off till he was sure it was right for both of them. . . .

Jackie said, "Listen, hon, I was just thinking. What I really need is a good, long, uninterrupted romantic night with Chris before I tell him Michael's coming home. We're going out Saturday night, and I think if I had a chance to really, really make him happy, he might come back, Michael or no Michael. So I'm not telling him about Michael, and don't you, either, okay?"

Jennifer smiled. "Cross my heart and hope to die, stick a needle in my eye. Mom, I didn't know you wanted Chris back all that much. I thought you were having a wonderful time being single and free and upwardly mobile and all that stuff."

Jackie's face changed for an instant, sagged and revealed age and strain. "I don't want to be alone when I'm old. You'll be gone pretty soon, and . . ." She shrugged. "Chris is about the sweetest, kindest guy I ever came across. And I can't blame him for being scared off by Michael. Do you think I'd have stayed in this household if I'd had any choice?"

"But yet you're trying to seduce poor Chris back into it? Knowing Michael is going to be here? Mom, that's not fair of you."

"I know it. Will you help me?"

Jennifer shrugged. "What do you want me to do? Just keep my mouth shut about Michael coming home?"

"That and. . . ," Jackie hesitated.

"Oh. Spend Saturday night at Kelly's, right? Sure."

After supper she tried to call Kelly but the line was busy, so she went outside and started toward Kelly's building. It was a clear, cool twilight, with stars just showing in the eastern sky. One star, low on the horizon, held her eye and brought music through her mind.

She stepped away from me and went through the fair, And fondly I watched her move here and move there, And then she went homeward with one star

80

awake, As the swan in the evening moves over the lake.

Guinevere heard John's soft, rich voice, felt the sensual folds of her gown around her legs.

She knew where she wanted to spend Saturday night.

Kelly opened the door, phone in her hand. "Gotta go, bye. Hi. I was just coming over to your place. You'll never guess who that was on the phone. You'll die. I'll die. Come on in."

In Kelly's overwhelmingly green bedroom, they sat cross-legged on the bed.

"That was Dennis Walker," Kelly said. "He called to ask me out Saturday, isn't that a kick? His family has a weekend place up on White Bear Lake and they have dances every Saturday night in this huge dance pavilion up there, with big-band music and long dresses and all that stuff. Isn't that wild? So, anyway, I'm going up with them for the weekend, but especially for the dance, and I have no idea what I've got that's good enough."

She bounced off the bed and rolled open the closet doors.

"Dennis Walker? My Dennis?" Jennifer said.

Kelly froze and turned. "I didn't know he was your Dennis. You never went out with him, did you?"

"No, I just always thought he liked me. He's my lab partner in physics, is all. No, I was just kidding. You can have him. He's a really nice guy."

"Well, the main thing is, he's the only son of Walker Buick, and you know they've got five dealerships now, just in the Twin Cities area alone. Dennis is going into the business."

"Ah-uh. Romance burns forever in your breast, doesn't it?"

Kelly turned from the closet with a handful of hangered dresses. "Listen, Jen, what burns in my breast is common sense. I want a beautiful house and a weekend place on White Bear and huge closets full of clothes. I'd be stupid not to use what I've got, while I've got it, to get what I want to get."

They laughed.

But when Jennifer went out into the night, she walked backward, slowly, until she found that one bright star low in the eastern sky.

Jackie looked up and said, "Are you all set for Saturday night, babe?"

In a somewhat distant voice, Jennifer said, "Kelly's got a date, so that's out. But don't worry. I've got a friend I can stay with at the fair. I'll just take my jammies and toothbrush with me Saturday morning."

"Thanks, Jen. You're a good kid. I'll try to get you a daddy out of the deal, okay?"

Jennifer waved a hand as she climbed the stairs. To herself she said, Don't worry about me. I'll be out of here for good. Maybe even before Michael comes. . . .

❧12❧

She woke before dawn to work on her hair. First a fragrant herbal shampoo, tedious minutes with the dryer, and then experiments before the bathroom mirror. The final result was a pile of dark curls twisted atop her head, with wisps and tendrils at her ears and neck. Instant maturity. Blue and white flowers circling the topknot and trailing in back added romance and innocence.

She wore the blue gown again, the one he'd first seen her in. Through the gauzy white billows of the sleeves, her arms showed as smooth and fascinating columns, hidden and revealed at once. The laces of the bodice lifted her breasts and rounded them above.

"He will love me tonight," she vowed. "He'll have to."

But there was the other world to get through first, the Toyota and the highway and the Saturday dawn traffic, motor homes and fishing boats going north to the lakes.

Dennis Walker and Kelly, going north to a pavilion dance on the lake. Jennifer tested herself for hurt and found none. Only John was important.

She was early through the virgin gate. Its keeper was just climbing the ladder to his perch, water bucket in hand. She waved and smiled, and passed beneath him.

Guinevere ran up the grassy avenue, eager for the fair. Life was boring in her father's castle, except for fair days in the village, and she'd been dreaming of the handsome young minstrel, dreaming of him in her tower room since the last fair day.

He was in his oak tree. She could see his feet dangling just above the round bench. Swiftly and silently she mounted the bench and came up into his arms. The kiss was spontaneous and natural as the dawning, and it deepened and hardened.

All the long morning he sang to her, ignoring the strangers from another century.

He sang in his deep, soft voice, "She laid her hand on me, and this she did say, It will not be long, love, Till our wedding day."

He sang, "Oh, my love is like a red, red rose that's sweetly sprung in June, Oh, my love is like a melody that's sweetly sung in tune. As fair thou art, my bonny lass, so deep in love am I, And I will love thee still, my dear, Till all the seas go dry."

Guinevere felt his words in the pit of her stomach. She was loved. Forever. Forever safe with his love around her like the piper's feather beds.

She left him when she had to, but his eyes were still on her, and she knew he was in her power.

At the afternoon jousts, Guinevere laughed and moved so merrily that the money poured into her tambourine. She led the tiny black stallion by his golden chain in the grand parade and in a moment of silliness sat on his back sideways. He toppled her with one buck jump that sent her legs aloft and spread her skirts on the ground. The men in the audience cheered, whistled, and hooted for more. The queen on her throne scowled.

Sir James the Incredibly Good won the fair Lady Guinevere in the final joust of the afternoon, defeating Sir Lawrence the Lover by halting his horse at the barrier, pointing out to Sir Lawrence a woman in the audience who was wearing a tank top and no bra. While Sir Lawrence was ogling, James dealt the telling blow and rode away to the barn with the fair Guinevere draped crossways over his horse's withers, feet kicking and arms waving for help.

John Lutanist watched from the edge of the crowd.

They met for supper at the inn, though they hadn't talked of it. John fetched the plates and carried them outside to a place just down the lane from the inn. Here the small stream that formed the ravine was diverted into a pool, with curved stone benches at its edge. White ducks swam there and profited from the sandwich crusts that came their way. Guinevere saw them as swans sailing over the lake.

They spoke little as they ate, Guinevere and John Lutanist, but they sat close together. His warmth touched her through her gown as a hand might, and excited her.

"I can't go home tonight," she said when the meal was done. "My mother . . . I told her I was staying with a friend at the fair. Am I?"

He lifted her hand and kissed her fingertips. "Of course, my lady," he whispered. "I am at your command."

"Nine o'clock, go home. Nine o'clock, go home."

In the far end of the horse barn were rest rooms with showers, where the knights could change into and out of their costumes. Guinevere bathed there. She stepped back into the blue gown and worked a few minutes to restore her hair and its flowers, then graciously gave the room over to the sweating knights.

Climbing the rise from the barn, she saw a group of people near Robert's hut. John was with them. He came to her side and took her hand.

"Robert invited us in for a jug of wine. Barf and Gagg are here, and a few of the other musicians. We can go in, or . . ."

She saw that he was freshly showered too, and nervous. Nervous about her, about her virginity? She smiled suddenly, a woman in control.

"Yes, let's go in for a little," Guinevere said. "I like Robert's wine."

The hut was too full of people for sitting. Guinevere had about her the glow of a bride, and it communicated itself to the others in wordless ways. Wine was mulled and passed, talk and jokes and laughter flowed around them, but Guinevere and John Lutanist were somehow central to the gathering.

Our bridal party, she thought. How did they know? But then in a village like ours, all is known. When Lady Guinevere takes the lute player to her heart and her bed, of course all the villagers sense it. And they wish us well.

Robert picked up his lap harp and plucked a merry tune, singing, "Step we gaily, off we go, heel for heel and toe for toe, Arm in arm and row on row, off to Mairi's wedding. Plenty herring, plenty meal, plenty peat to fill her creel, Plenty bonny bairns as well, That's our toast for Mairi. . . ."

He sang to the room, but his eye cut slyly toward Guinevere.

It was a wonderful wedding party, she thought as John led her through the night. And now . . .

The trailer was a jarring note. It should have been a cottage with hollyhocks and roses. But the trailer was only dimly lit, and there were flowers on the table, flowers of blue and white like those in her hair. He had prepared the bower for her coming.

His touch was a poet's touch, sensitive and sure.

*   *   *

They slept holding each other, her dark hair a blanket for his chest. She woke in the night and thought, Now I'm safe. Now I'm his.

John woke in the night and thought, "She was my dream and a vision divine, until I kissed her and took her to me." And what have I done to her now, this lovely, trusting child? What have I done to her?

13

Jennifer woke disoriented. She opened her eyes and found John raised on one elbow beside her, studying her face. Although she smiled, she felt oddly resentful, as though he'd been spying on her.

She had given him the gift that can be offered only once, her innocence, and now in some obscure way she felt shortchanged.

Later, as she sat on the edge of the bed he asked, "Are you sorry, my lady?"

"I'm not your lady, I'm myself. Jennifer, not Guinevere." She hadn't meant to snap.

"Jennifer. Are you having regrets? You wanted this as much as I did, you know."

"Yes, I know. And I'm not having regrets exactly."

"Then what exactly? You don't seem very happy."

She looked away from him, out the window. How

89

could she say, "You don't love me enough. I gave you more than you're giving me"?

Diffidently she said, "Last night you said you loved me. I just wondered how much you meant that, or was it just something men always say."

John smiled. "Some of both, Jennie. I meant it when I was saying it, but maybe not in the way you want me to mean it. You know what my life is. You know I'm a loner by nature."

"And I'm just one of your groupies, right?" She tried for a note of casual lightness and fell short.

"No. Of course you're not." He pulled her down against him and held her, stroking her hair. "You are very special and very precious to me, and at this moment you're the love of my life. But . . . I don't want you to be hurt, sweetheart. That's why I was holding off. I didn't want you building up unrealistic expectations about me, that's all. I love you to the best of my ability, given my nature. Do you understand that?"

She sighed, and after a long time she nodded against his chest.

"Now, then," he said more briskly, "what would you like for breakfast?"

It was a beautiful morning, clear and crisp. The sumac that grew along the ravine was dark red and the aspens' leaves a buttery gold.

John and Jennifer crossed the ravine hand in hand and took their place under the village square oak tree. He tuned his lute strings and sang, "Alas, my love, you do me wrong, To cast me off discourteously, For I have loved you, oh, so long, Delighting in your company."

Jennifer sat and smiled as she listened, but the music failed to weave its old spell. This morning, she saw John as a somewhat aging musician who played pretend games for a living.

It occurred to her that he, too, had risked much and offered much last night. And perhaps he felt a loss this morning also.

He waited until she had left, and then he sang almost too softly to draw an audience, "She was a woman then, woman of mine, With a voice and a touch and a need of her own. She was a woman then, less than divine, And the dream I had loved, of her, oh, it was flown."

They met for supper at the inn and once again took their plates outdoors to the benches by the duck pond. There was an ease between them now, an acknowledgment of the bond that held them, and of the flaws in that bond. She hoped he would ask her to come to the trailer during the week, but he didn't and she accepted that. He kissed her lightly, and they went their separate ways.

With an hour to kill before the first of the evening's jousts, Jennifer wandered through the stock market and beyond, toward Robert's hut. He was sitting on his stump stool outside the hut, playing a haunting pipe tune. She sat on the grass and waited for it to end.

"I see you're wearing the same dress you were wearing last night," Robert said without greeting, as he set the bagpipe's chanter aside.

"A gentleman wouldn't notice," she said.

"I stand corrected." He cocked her a knowing look with a smile inside it.

They sat silently for a few minutes. Then Robert said, "Did you come to talk about John or just to drive away my paying customers with your long, sad face?"

"Is it? Long and sad?"

"Aye, lass, it is."

"You can cut the accent, Robert. This is the real world now, you know."

"A bit too real for you, is it now, Jennifer? You spent the night with the minstrel lad, did you not? Was it an unhappy experience then?"

"No, it was great. Well . . ."

"Not unhappy exactly, but not up to expectations, is that it? Our expectations are often our downfall, girl. Don't expect the man to be something he's not. 'Tisn't fair to either of you."

"I know that," she said testily.

"Well, then." Robert smiled his dear smile. "You're very young, if you don't mind me saying so. Young can be charming, don't get me wrong. But young is . . . shall I tell you where I think the dividing line lies between youth and adult?"

"Not when you lose your virginity, right?" Her voice was deep, teasing.

Robert laughed and inadvertently squeezed a wail

92

from his bagpipe. "No, that's got little or nothing to do with it, as I'm sure you know. Adults are people who understand the connection between their decisions and the consequences of 'em."

"Taking responsibility, you mean?"

"Something like that, yes, but it's more, well, just understanding the chain of events, do you see?"

"No."

"Well, then, if I explained it to you, you'd be riding on the coattails of my maturity, wouldn't you? Not developing your own."

Jennifer kindled to this man, to his wisdom and the merry, compassionate gleam in his eye. "I like you, Robert."

"Ah, now," he warned, "don't be saying things like that or I may wake up dead one of these mornings with a lute wrapped around my neck."

Michael. Today was the day Michael came home. In another two hours, she would have to walk into her house and face him, face her terror of his power and his violence. The fifteenth century would fade behind her. It wasn't going to protect her from Michael.

Robert's face sobered. "What is it, Jennifer? What did I say? You've gone pale. John's not going to brain me with his lute; it's too valuable. I was only joking."

"My brother's coming home today," she said. "He's been in a correctional facility since he was seventeen, for uncontrolled violent behavior. They think they've cured him with hormone treatments, but I don't believe it. I'm scared to death of him, Robert.

So is my mom. So was my stepdad, but he got out. Mom and I can't get out of it. Michael is ours; we have to have him. I don't want to go home tonight, Robert."

He asked for details and she told him everything about Michael, the exploded frog and the drowned parakeet, and Kelly's injured breast. She described the knife point against her throat and her mother's. Fair visitors wandered slowly past, seeing the Scottish piper and hoping for a pipe tune, but Robert ignored them and sat listening intently. He leaned forward on his stump, hands clasped hard between his kilted legs.

When she finished he was silent, thoughtful. Finally he said, "And so you've gone to John Turnbull to protect you from the ugly reality at home, haven't you?"

Jennifer shook her head. "No. It wasn't that. We were just attracted to each other right from the first."

"Ah." He cradled the bagpipe, expertly flipping its long drone pipes over his shoulder and setting his fingers over the chanter's holes.

"John Turnbull is a good man," he said gently. "He's not a marrying man, but he's honest, I think. Trust him, Jennifer, my love, but don't mistake him for what he's not. And think about what I said before. Actions and reactions. We all create our own lives, you know."

She grinned at him. "Which course did you learn that in?"

94

"Buddhist philosophy, I believe it was. Or Chilean literature."

She rose and kissed the top of his head. "This has been delightful, professor, but I have to go be a prize in a jousting tournament. Thanks for caring."

He watched her walk away and shook his head. John wasn't good enough for that girl, he thought.

14

It was not quite nine-thirty when Jennifer opened the townhouse door and stepped into an unfamiliar living room. Furniture cluttered the walking space, cartons and suitcases stood everywhere, and the air was charged with the energy of a stranger.

Jackie and Michael were in the small room off the living room, where Jackie's office had been. Her desk, files, and computer equipment cluttered the living room. Taking their place were a new twin-size bed of light oak and a dresser to match.

Jackie was holding the headboard while Michael wrestled the side pieces of the bed frame into their slots. He looked so handsome, so pleasant. So normal. Was it possible that he might be okay now?

"Hi, babe," Jackie called. Michael looked over his

shoulder warily, as though he were anxious about her reaction to his presence.

"Hi, Mom. Michael. Welcome home."

"Come give us a hand after you get out of your costume," Jackie said. "We went out to Slumberland after supper and got this stuff. I wanted Michael to pick out what he wanted. You can help us with the mattress and springs, okay?"

Happy family, that's the role we're playing, Jennifer thought as she changed from Guinevere's blue gown to her old jeans and sweatshirt. Okay, I'll go along. I just hope Michael does.

The three of them wrestled the mattress and springs into place. Then Jackie and Jennifer flung the new sheets out between them and smoothed them over the bed. Michael began unpacking his shirts and underwear into the dresser drawers.

Jackie went into the kitchen and came back with a Supervalue birthday cake, alight, in her hands. She started a forced song. "Happy birthday to you, happy birthday to you, happy birthday, dear . . ."

The doorbell rang, startling them all. Ten o'clock on a Sunday night?

"Must be Kelly," Jennifer said.

But it was Chris. He stood in the door with a wine bottle in his hand, staring at the confusion of office furniture in the living room.

"Chris," Jackie said stupidly.

"Come on in." Jennifer waved him through the door.

He said, "I thought I'd take a chance and surprise you. . . . Your lights were on . . . Michael?"

Michael towered in the arch between the rooms. "Hi, Dad." He used the word as an insult.

"I didn't know. . . ," Chris foundered.

Brightly Jackie said, "Michael's home for good. I picked him up this afternoon, and we've been out shopping for bedroom furniture. Come and see what we got. We're fixing this up in here for Michael, see? They had these oak sets on sale, thirty percent off. That dresser was only a hundred eighty-nine ninety-five, down from, I forget, two hundred something. We were just going to have birthday cake and coffee. It's Michael's twenty-first birthday, isn't it, honey?"

"Yeah," Michael said. His eyes hadn't left Chris.

Chris set the wine bottle down on the coffee table and looked at Jackie with an expression of bewilderment and rising anger. "You never said anything about this, Jack. All that last night, and you had to know he was being released today, and you never said one word about it to me."

Jackie's mouth opened, her hands motioned helplessly in the air, but no words came out.

Michael said, "I can see I'm real welcome in this household. New bed and dresser, big hairy deal. Nobody wants me here. Well, I don't want to be here, either."

Jackie said, "I'm sorry, Chris. I wanted to tell you, I tried to tell you, but . . ."

"No, you didn't," Chris said flatly. "You thought if

I didn't know it, you'd have me back again. Didn't you? Didn't you?"

"No, Chris, that's not true. Wait, listen."

"Well, it almost worked, lady. I came over here tonight . . . look, I brought champagne and everything. I was going to get here early, before Jen got home, so we could have some time alone, and I was going to propose. Only my battery was dead and I had to get my neighbor to jump-start the car, so I was a little late."

Embarrassment lay thick in the air of the room. Michael turned abruptly and slammed out through the front door. Held breaths escaped.

Jackie flared first. "That was a tactful thing to do to him, his first night home. You really made him feel wanted, Chris. Now he thinks he's spoiling things between you and me."

Jennifer retreated around the desk and files, and climbed the stairs to her room, but the voices followed her, too loud to be shut out.

"Why didn't you tell me he was coming home? Huh? Why? Just tell me that. Not that I'll believe anything you say, you bitch."

Jennifer sickened. She'd never heard Chris talk that way, not even in the worst of the bad times before.

"Honey, listen, I was going to tell you. But last night was so perfect, and I knew it was going to be the last chance we'd have to be really alone together. I guess I just hated to break the mood. I'm sorry."

"What were you going to do, hide him in the attic every evening when I came home from work, and let him out in the morning? What were you thinking of, Jackie? You wanted me to marry you again, didn't you?"

The answer came too low for Jennifer to hear.

"Well, then couldn't you have been honest with me? Couldn't you have trusted me? We probably could have worked it out some way, about Michael. But no, you had to try to lie to me about it."

"I didn't . . ."

"The same thing as. I'm sorry, Jackie, I just can't do this again. I can't live in the same house with Michael. I'm not going to go through that again. Find yourself another . . ."

A muffled pause, a quietly closed door, and Jackie's running step on the stairs.

Jennifer went into her mother's room and took her shaking shoulders and held her. They cried together, for different men.

Later they sat in the kitchen eating birthday cake and drinking the champagne Chris had left. In the natural aftermath of the tears, they laughed.

"You know what?" Jackie said suddenly. "I wish this was olden times and that you were deformed or ugly or something."

Jennifer laughed loudly. "Is there a reason for that wish, or just general nastiness?"

"No, listen, if it were olden times and you were really ugly, maybe a little off in the head, then you'd

100

have to stay at home all your life and take care of your saintly old gray-haired mother. You'd be the unmarriageble daughter, and that's what old-maid daughters did. It must have been great for the old folks. Get waited on hand and foot, never have to worry about getting warehoused in a retirement home . . ."

"Oh, come now. You're not worrying about your old age. Just because Chris didn't take the bait. If you really want to get married again, you'll find somebody."

"I know," Jackie sighed. "It's just that, well, times like this I realize how much I depend on you to hold things together. I really screwed up with Chris, didn't I?"

Jennifer thought about Robert and what he'd said about actions and reactions and assuming responsibility for them. "Well, it was sort of your own fault, Mom. You did make the decision to try to get Chris hooked before you told him about Michael, so you have to accept the fact that you ran a risk of it backfiring. It did backfire, but it was your own fault for creating the situation in the first place. See?"

"My, you've gotten wise all of a sudden." Jackie poured another glass of champagne. "How was your night last night, by the way? Who'd you stay with?"

Jennifer looked at the stove. Should she tell the truth, or would it be a bad time for that much honesty? "This friend of mine. She's a fair maiden, too. Rides a horse sidesaddle."

Jackie looked at her long and hard, until Jennifer turned and met her gaze. "She," Jackie said.

101

Jennifer flushed and looked away again.

With a long sigh, Jackie tipped up the empty bottle. "Well, my dear, you are not deformed or touched in the head. It was bound to happen sooner or later. I'm not sure I'm ready to think about this, not tonight, anyway. Jen?"

"What?"

"Are you okay?"

"Yes, saintly old gray-haired mother. I'm fine. I'm fine really."

"Are you being careful?"

Jennifer stood abruptly. "I'm fine and I'm being careful, and I'm going to bed. Coming?"

"No. I'll wait up for Michael. He really shouldn't be . . ."

"Wandering around loose at night?"

Their eyes met.

She lay in bed exhausted, but her mind wouldn't slow down. Careful? No, they hadn't been careful. Insane that now, twenty-four hours after the fact, she was just realizing the risk she'd taken.

Pregnancy.

Deadly diseases too terrible to think about.

John lived a loose and mobile existence. There were bound to have been other women, possibly carrying infections.

Tears gathered in the corners of her eyes. John hadn't protected her.

He hadn't protected her.

15

In the days that followed, Jennifer found it almost impossible to concentrate on her schoolwork. High school, even from senior-status level, was simply not the real world. The real world was a fifteenth-century English village and a warm-eyed minstrel in an oak tree.

The only part of high school that held any immediacy for Jennifer was the need for keeping up her grade average for college entrance requirements, and with every weekend night spent with John, that need receded. College was no longer the definite block of future waiting for her after this final high-school year. College and whatever career it led to were beginning to feel like someone else's dream, not Jennifer's.

All week Jennifer dreamed about him, counted off

the days until the weekend, and yet when she was finally alone with him, the words he murmured were never quite enough for her.

She began to comprehend that John was less intelligent than she was, in spite of his wider experience in the world. When they sat together in Robert's hut for wine and talk after the fair closed for the night, it was Jennifer who understood Robert's subtle humor more quickly. There were times, in fact, when she felt that the coupling was wrong, that she and Robert were the mates.

With Robert there was always talk, stimulating ideas to be explored and life to be looked at through his ironic, philosophical view. With John there were silences, held hands and kissed fingertips, and long, warm looks.

He sang her love ballads, but he made no offer of a life together.

On the Wednesday before the last of the fair's weekends, Jennifer's fourth-hour study period was interrupted by a request that she come to the counselor's office.

"Sit down, Jennifer. It's nothing serious. I just wanted to talk to you a little bit about your grades."

Miss Janeck looked like a student herself and dressed like one. Jennifer felt comfortable with her.

"I know," Jennifer sighed. "They've been slipping a little bit lately, but I can get them up again."

"The question is, will you? Is something bothering you at home or in your private life? I don't like to pry, but when outside problems affect a student with a grade average like yours, especially with the competition there is nowadays to get into good colleges . . ."

"I know it. I'll try harder."

"Jennifer? You didn't answer my question. Is there something wrong at home?"

"Well, my brother . . ." And she told Miss Janeck the situation. While the counselor made sympathetic, supportive comments and assured Jennifer that her door was open anytime she wanted to talk, Jennifer knew that Michael was the smaller part of the distraction that prevented her from concentrating on her work.

She drove home after school only half listening to Kelly, who was in love by now with Dennis and his family's business and seldom stayed on any other topic very long. It would have been a relief for Jennifer if she could talk to someone about John, but there was no one. Her mother had enough to handle right now; Kelly was engrossed with her own love life; school counselors had only brief slices of time and were oriented toward getting those college bound launched, not toward advice to the lovelorn.

With relief she waved Kelly off, in the driveway, and turned toward her own front door. Then she froze.

From beyond the door came the blood-chilling bellow of Michael enraged. There was a loud crash and a thin scream.

"Kelly," Jennifer yelled. "Call the police! Michael!"

She ran for the door and pulled it open. Jackie lay on the floor near the sofa; Michael stood over her, legs splayed, arms high in a grotesque parody of the Jolly Green Giant. In his hands he held the computer terminal, as big and heavy as a television set.

The room was a tornado path of overturned furniture and computer paper, yards of it pulled across the wreckage.

Jackie lay still, blood pouring from her nose. As the computer dropped, Jennifer screamed and lunged toward Michael.

He turned on her, his face dark red and distorted with rage. His hands reached for her throat.

"No," she screamed.

She stumbled and fell toward him. His fingers closed around her throat and squeezed.

I'm going to die now, she realized. A whirlpool of red and black enveloped her head and pulled her down into a universal silence.

She was distantly aware of bagpipe music, or was it a siren? And voices and jostling movement. Then nothing again until she woke in a hospital room. Kelly's mother sat beside her bed, holding her hand.

"You awake?" Mrs. Green asked gently. "You're going to be fine, Jennie, honey. And your mom's going to be fine, too, so you just relax."

When Jennifer tried to speak, her throat swelled with pain and closed against the effort. With tears pooling in her eyes, she motioned toward her neck.

106

"The nurse will be here in a minute," Mrs. Green said. "Your neck is bruised pretty bad, but nothing broken. And you banged your head when you fell, so they're watching you for concussion, but they don't think you've got anything to worry about on that score."

Jennifer formed the word *Mom* with her lips.

"They're taking X rays now. She was beaten up pretty badly, honey, but the doctors don't think there is any brain damage or internal injuries. They think she's got some broken ribs and missing teeth . . . and one eye . . ."

Jennifer stared.

"One eye that will have to be replaced, honey, but they do wonderful things nowadays with prophylactic eyes. You honestly can't tell them from the real thing. And she'll be able to work and everything."

Tears coursed from the corners of her eyes and down, wetting her hair and pillow.

"Hate . . . him," she whispered. It caused agony in her throat, but it had to be said.

Mrs. Green patted her arm. "I don't blame you one bit, sweetie. The Bible says we should never hate our fellow human beings, but just between you and me, I think sometimes we should, when they do things like this. I never could forgive that boy for what he did to Kelly that time, hurting her breast. That was a terrible thing to do and I don't care how many psychologists say, 'He's sick, he has problems, he can't help himself.' All I know is he does terrible things to innocent people, and that ought not to be

107

allowed. I shouldn't be talking this way to you, I know. . . ."

Jennifer shook her head, smiled, and gripped the woman's hand. Mrs. Green was saying exactly what Jennifer needed to have said.

By the next day, Jennifer was home from the hospital and Michael was in the Hennepin County Jail, awaiting his hearing. When the lawyer asked him why he'd attacked his mother and sister he said, "My mother had it coming. They turned me down for a job at Three M, and I went home and told her I couldn't get a job, and she told me I had to because I couldn't live with her forever. And she *had* a job. She *had a job*," he screamed. "They wouldn't give me a job, but everybody else had one. She had a job and money, and it was her house so she could just tell me she didn't want me to live there, and I couldn't live anyplace else because I didn't have any money, because *they wouldn't give me that job*."

"Why did you attack your sister?"

Michael didn't remember doing that. He didn't remember Jennifer's being there at all.

All day Thursday Jennifer rested on the sofa with cold packs on her throat and Mrs. Green popping in to see if she needed anything. The Greens had both come over the night before and straightened the furniture up and cleared away the tangled yards of computer paper. The computer itself, broken and blood smeared, they set back on its table.

Through the afternoon and evening, after Kelly finally left, Jennifer cried weakly for herself, for Jackie . . . and for John, whom she needed. He didn't know she'd been hurt; she couldn't blame him for not being there. But she needed him, nonetheless, and resented him for not knowing and not coming.

And Robert. How wonderful it would be to have Robert's clear-eyed compassion.

She tried to call Chris, to tell him Jackie was in the hospital, but there was no answer. She left the message on his machine, but didn't hope for much from him.

On Friday morning she woke knowing that she couldn't go on. Michael had nearly killed her mother and herself, and it would happen again. They would lock him up for a while and give him therapy and hormone treatments and turn him loose again, and he would come back. Always, he would come back.

"I can't stand it. I won't stay here."

She drove to the hospital after a liquid breakfast; her throat still couldn't take solid food. Jackie was heavily bandaged, tubed, and sedated. Jennifer sat with her for an hour, till her mother drifted off to sleep. Then she walked faster and faster through the hospital, half ran across the parking lot, and turned the Toyota toward the southbound freeway.

Toward the fifteenth century.

❧ 16 ❧

She drove through the Quik-Trip and onto the dirt track behind it. At the edge of the camping area, she parked and walked self-consciously among the trailers and motor homes.

It was late afternoon and cooling noticeably. In the woods beyond the trailers, the oaks were dull red-brown against the bright yellow of the poplars and the deep black-green of the pines. Underfoot the grass was brown and crisp.

John's trailer was empty. She knocked but knew from the absence of music within that he wasn't there. Then she heard the voice of the lute through the trees behind her. She turned and moved down the bank of the ravine, toward the song.

At the edge of the clearing, she stopped to look at him and to listen. He sat on the edge of the rough plank stage of the Ash Grove theater. The stump and board seats were empty on the grassy slope beyond him, but three large gray squirrels moved among the seats. They had work to do, transporting acorns up into the huge old oaks that were their province; they had no time to wait for the man to leave.

It was a song Jennifer hadn't heard before, a lovely, sad minor-key melody. He sang the words so softly that she knew he was singing to an ache inside himself.

"She was a dream, a vision of mine, Born of my loneliness, born from my need. She was my dream and a vision divine, Until I kissed her and took her to me.

"She was a woman then, woman of mine, with a voice and a touch and a need of her own. She was a woman then, less than divine, and the dream I had loved, of her, oh, it was flown.

"For I kissed her and took her to me, to me, For I kissed her and took her to me. . . ."

It wasn't just a song he sang. She knew that, and it broke something deep within her. John didn't want the reality of her in his life. He wanted the romantic dream, that was all. Not the everyday living. Not Jennifer Dean, whole person.

Silently she backed away from the clearing. Across the ravine she felt her way up the bank, her eyes blurred with unshed tears. She started through the trailers toward her car, but hesitated as a dusty Bronco pulled up beside it and parked.

Robert got out, reached into the back for bags of groceries, then straightened when he saw her. She stood with an awkward kind of grace in her jeans and big-necked sweater. Purple bruises stained her neck and temple, and her eyes had blue shadows beneath them. Her hair was uncombed, forgotten all day.

He dropped the bags and took her into his arms in a swoop of unthinking compassion.

"Jennie. What's happened?"

She shook her head and burrowed against him to cry. He held her and stroked her back, her hair. "Aw, aw," he said, sounding as though he might cry himself. It was exactly what she needed.

When the worst was over, she helped him carry the grocery bags to his hut, where he set them aside as unimportant, and took her to the feather beds and sat beside her to hold her again.

"Was it John? Did you break up? What happened to your head? Can you tell me about it, or do you just want to cry some more?"

"You are so sweet," she said, snuffling and hiccuping.

"Was it your brother?"

She nodded and told him about Michael's attack. "I don't know why I came out here this afternoon. I wanted to see John and tell him what happened. . . . I needed . . ."

Robert stroked her hair.

"I needed for him to help me some way. Protect me or save me from the whole mess at home. You know?"

She felt him nodding.

"What did he say when you told him?"

"I didn't. He was singing, over at the Ash Grove, practicing, I thought, and I went over there to tell him. I guess I wanted him to say he'd marry me and take me with him." She laughed a small, sad laugh. "Or at least take me with him. I wanted . . . something.

"But he was singing this song about me, about loving the dream of me but the dream was flown when he kissed me and took me to him. Why does it have to be like that, Robert? It's crazy. You love somebody and all you want is to be with them and make love to them, and then as soon as it happens, it's like it's all over. Why? Why doesn't it get better and better?"

They shifted back on the bed until their backs were against the hut's wall. She settled her head into the hollow of his neck and nourished herself against his solid warmth.

"Because," Robert said in his soft, smile-lightened voice. "Because, Jennie, it never was real, that's why. You didn't love John Turnbull. You didn't know John Turnbull. You had no idea what the man was really all about, nor did he know Jennifer Dean. You fell in love with the music, the dream. The wandering minstrel from another century. Admit it now, you did."

She was silent.

"I know John a little bit, from the years we've been working this fair together. There's almost always a pretty girl at every fair. He doesn't bed them usually,

I'm not saying that. In fact, you're the first I've know of that he's taken it that far with. But he falls in love with them. Romantically. He writes songs about them and daydreams about them, and never sees them again. And, listen to me, Jennifer"—he took her chin in his fingers and raised her face—"he wants it that way. He *wants* it that way. It's his nature."

She dropped her head and nodded against him, and he played with the strands of her hair.

"You know," he said, "back in the days of knights and ladies and minstrels, that was pretty much the way society worked. People married for reasons of property, security, titles. No one expected to find romance within marriage. The men had wives to provide heirs, and they had their romances elsewhere. The fine ladies had lovely flirtations with their husbands' knights and squires and pages . . . and minstrels, and that was considered natural."

"I didn't know that," she murmured.

"Sure. And it probably was a system more in keeping with human nature than our expectations of marriage and monogamy. The point is, John Turnbull truly is a man born out of his time. He has the soul of a wandering minstrel, and he loves in the way that men loved then. The lady is a distant object to be worshiped and desired. She's not to be lived with in an everyday way. Do you understand any of this?"

After a long pause, Jennifer nodded again. "You're right, of course. It wasn't really him I fell in love with. It couldn't have been. He was just a face, a song. What I fell in love with," she said slowly, thinking her way through it, "what I fell in love with was my own idea of him, what I needed him to be. Like I was projecting onto a movie screen or something. It was coming out of me, not out of him. Wasn't it?"

"I'm afraid so." He held her tightly for a moment, bolstering her.

"And what John fell in love with was a fair maiden. Just that. Nothing about the real Jennifer Dean. He saw a girl dancing in a long blue dress and that . . . connected . . . with something in him that he needed. But it wasn't me really."

Understanding flooded through her and set her back at a distance from the pain. John Turnbull began to slip into perspective; her first love—but an episode only. And it was over now. She would see him again, maybe love him again, but she was beyond her need for him.

When Robert moved to stand up, she said in a low, smiling voice, "You're not going to sing me a song, are you?"

He laughed. "No. I expect there's been enough of that already. Probably too much. What I had in mind was a pot of chili with a whole mess of cheese melted over it. Will you stay and dine with me?"

She snuffled and smiled and wiped her face with the cowl of her sweater. "I have to get back to the hospital pretty soon, but I think I could eat a little chili and cheese."

❧17❧

Sunday morning. Sparkling October air and a glitter of frost on the ground. The walled city rose before her.

She lifted the skirt of the red-and-gold gown and walked swiftly through the gate. Her carriage was the erect grace of a nobly born lady.

"Virgins only, through this gate," the guard's voice came down from the high wall. "Imposters gets boiling oil poured on them."

Jennifer started as usual toward the third gate but caught herself, looked up at the guard, and, grinning, swerved to another gate. He laughed at her and waved her away.

She sat at the feet of the tree-borne minstrel but didn't stand up to him for a kiss. He looked at her sadly and sang.

116

"Hushed be thy moaning, lone bird of the sea, Rocks are a home and a shelter to thee. Thine is the angry wave, mine but the lonely grave. Ho ro, mairidhu, turn ye to me."

He sang, "When I'm lonely, dear white heart, Black the night or wild the sea, By love's light my foot finds the old pathway to thee. Thou art the music of my heart, Harp of joy, oh cruit mo chridh, Moon of guidance by night, Strength and light thou art to me."

"You're singing sad songs today, minstrel," Guinevere said.

He looked at her with love and loss in his eyes. "Yes," he said simply.

"Nine o'clock, go home, come again next year," the village crier called, swinging his lantern as he strode through the stock market. Already most of the animals were gone, the camels and the elephants and the donkey with her woolly baby.

Jennifer rode astride on Spotless, behind Sir James the Incredibly Good, who was easing out of his headgear and turning into Jim Blank, insurance underwriter and weekend horsemen. They rode somewhat aimlessly through the stock market and up the dark lanes of the village, reluctant to let go of it all. Other knights rode, too, and the sidesaddle maiden on her gray palfrey.

In most of the tiny shops along the lanes, unmedieval electric lights burned while artisans and shopkeepers packed their wares in crates. Vans and

117

pickups, driven in through the virgin gate, jammed the narrow lanes to receive the crates, the racks of homespun clothes, the cartons of handmade boots. Small impromptu parties sprung up everywhere—a few bottles, some bags of chips, plastic glasses to receive the splash of wine or beer from the Quik-Trip.

Jim said, "Let's get out of this traffic," and headed the horse toward the stock market and the long barn beyond the jousting field.

The barn was alight and alive. All but a few of the horses had been trucked away earlier in the evening, and the stall partitions had been broken down and moved aside. Knights in every stage of dress from armor to underwear were there, and their wives and children. Jerry, the announcer, moved through the crowd, joking and slapping backs.

Jennifer recognized faces from the stock market, the concession operators and the horse trader and the elephant and camel men. Robert was there in rather startling magnificence, wearing the formal full-dress kilt, with black velvet jacket and frothy lace shirt, and a sporran pouch of white fur hanging over his stomach.

As she slid from the horse's rump, Jennifer saw John coming from the shadows to catch her. Lightly he held her and kissed her. Then, with an awkward motion, he pulled something from under his arm and wrapped it around her.

It was one of the breathtakingly lovely cashmere shawls from the weavers' stall at the edge of the stock market. Cloud white it was and cloud soft against her cheek. The night was chill, and the wool gave a loving warmth to her.

"Thank you, John." Her words were deeply meant and as deeply felt by the man who stood before her.

"Will you stay with me tonight?" he asked.

She considered it, had considered it throughout the day. Last night she had left the fair at nine for a fast visit to the hospital. She'd told John about Michael's attack when she'd arrived Saturday morning, and he'd been warmly sympathetic and concerned. He hadn't pressed her to stay with him that night, but now he asked. Now would be their last chance together. . . .

"There'd be no point in it, would there?" she asked sadly, smiling.

"Point? No, I suppose no point, but . . . I'm going to miss you, my lady."

"I'll miss you. You were an important part of my life, John Lutanist."

"Turnbull," he corrected.

"Too late now for realism, though, isn't it? You didn't want it before, when I needed . . . oh, well, no use in going into that. It was a lovely fantasy. And I think," she said with a note of wonder in her voice, "I think that probably you were the right man for me just then, John. I think you were what I needed. I didn't want my first . . . time . . . to be with some silly boy in a parked car or . . . like that . . . you know."

"A trailer was better?" His eyes twinkled.

"Yes, because you made it lovely for me. It was a

119

fantasy for both of us, but if I'm pregnant or caught a disease or something, then that's going to be extremely real. But even if that happens, it's my responsibility, not yours. I want you to know that."

A look of immense relief and lightness came over his face. He held her close and murmured into her hair. "You've given me a great gift, Jennifer. I'll never forget you, as long as I live."

He kissed her one last, long, sad kiss and went off into the night. As she turned to enter the barn, she heard him singing.

Within the barn the air was alive with voices and movement. Dust motes rose in the lantern light and couples danced to a jig tune.

It came from Robert, who sat on a table with the beer keg and a clutter of opened chip bags. He picked at the lap harp that lay over his sporran, and at the top of his lungs he sang:

"If a body meet a body, comin' through the rye, If a body kiss a body, need a body cry? Every laddie has his lassie, None they say have I, Yet all the girls they smile on me when comin' through the rye."

He waved Jennifer to him and happily she went.

DATE DUE

DEC 2 0			
JAN 1 5			
FEB 1 0			
FEB 2 6			
MAR 1 0			
MAY 2 1			
MAY 1 4			

F
Hal   Hall, Lynn.
        Fair maiden